What do you look for in a guy? Charisma.
Sex appeal. Confidence. A body to die for.
Looks that stand out from the crowd. Well,
look no further—this brand-new collection has
four guys with all this—and more! And now
that they've met the women in these novels,
there is one thing on everyone's mind....

NIGHTS OF PASSION

One night is never enough!

The guys know what they want and how
they're going to get it!

Don't miss any of these hot stories, where
electrifying romance and sizzling passion are
guaranteed!

The Tycoon's Virgin
Susan Stephens

Bedded for Diamonds
Kelly Hunter

His for the Taking
Julie Cohen

Purchased for Pleasure
Nicola Marsh

Dear Reader,

Welcome to February's NIGHTS OF PASSION collection, featuring four brand-new, passionate novels. These offer more of what you love—strong, sexy alpha heroes; dramatic, sizzling, sexy story lines and a variety of exciting backdrops from around the world. In this collection, all four stories feature NIGHTS OF PASSION—*one night is never enough!*

If you love a millionaire—or a billionaire, for that matter—check out our next collection, TAKEN BY THE MILLIONAIRE, available March 2008. Find out what happens when these ordinary women enter the glamorous world of the superrich....

We'd love to hear what you think. E-mail us at Presents@hmb.co.uk or find more information about books and authors at www.iheartpresents.com.

With best wishes,

The Editors

HIS FOR THE TAKING

JULIE COHEN

NIGHTS OF PASSION

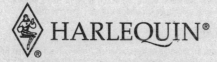

HARLEQUIN®

TORONTO • NEW YORK • LONDON
AMSTERDAM • PARIS • SYDNEY • HAMBURG
STOCKHOLM • ATHENS • TOKYO • MILAN • MADRID
PRAGUE • WARSAW • BUDAPEST • AUCKLAND

ISBN-13: 978-0-373-82069-6
ISBN-10:   0-373-82069-0

HIS FOR THE TAKING

First North American Publication 2008.

Previously published in the U.K. under the title DRIVING HIM WILD.

www.eHarlequin.com

Printed in U.S.A.

JULIE COHEN was born in the U.S.A and brought up in the mountains of western Maine. There wasn't much going on in Maine, so she made stuff up. She spent most of her childhood with her nose in a book. After gaining her first degree in English literature, she moved to England and researched fairies in children's literature for a postgraduate degree. She started writing her first Harlequin® romance novel on a blueberry farm in Maine, and finished it on a beach in Greece. Shortly after being chosen as a finalist in the Romance Writers of America's Golden Heart contest, she sold her first novel to Harlequin®.

Julie lives in the U.K. with her husband, who works in the music industry, and their baby son. She still reads everything in sight, and her other hobbies include walking, traveling, listening to loud music, watching films and eating far too much popcorn. She teaches secondary-school English and is teased daily about her American accent. Visit her Web site at www.julie-cohen.com, and write to her at julie-cohen@ntlworld.com.

For the inspiration behind Xenia Drake,
my grandmother Lillian Cohen.

I'll always miss you.

CHAPTER ONE

HE'D BEEN SITTING here so long his rear end was starting to go numb.

Nick shifted his weight, stretched his legs in their lightweight outdoor trousers, settled his back more comfortably against the tastefully neutral-coloured wall, and then he was motionless again.

There was a clock on the wall down the corridor from him, near the creaky elevators. It ticked in the emptiness, a constant artificial monotony that dragged on Nick's nerves. It wasn't the noise that bothered him. He was used to noise back home: the constant rush of the ocean and the whirr of leaves and the bickering of birds. Those were timeless sounds. But this tick was a precise measurement of time passing. Every second ticking by was another second he had to wait for the mysterious Ms Drake and the answers he'd waited far too long for already.

He glanced at his watch; it was over two hours since he'd spoken with the uniformed concierge in the fancy lobby downstairs.

If Nick hadn't known he was in New York already from the traffic and the blare and the buildings and the stink, he would've known from that guy. Surely nowhere else in the world could someone whose job it was to welcome people to a building be so hostile. As soon as Nick had walked in the building the concierge had been glaring at him.

Nick had ignored it, of course, striding across the marble floor straight to the art deco elevator and punching the up button.

'Can I help you, sir?' The words dripped with condescension, especially the last one.

'No. I know where I'm going.' Nick stared straight ahead at the bronze elevator grille.

'Staying for a while, are you?'

Nick didn't answer. Maybe if he ignored the man he would go away.

No luck. The man's next words came from behind his shoulder.

'That's a very large backpack.'

The large pointer above the elevators crawled slowly down the dial from the tenth floor towards the ground floor.

'What apartment are you visiting? Or are you moving in?'

The sarcasm made him finally turn to face the concierge. Nick was a good half a foot taller than the guy and much broader and he knew for a fact he was radiating anger. The concierge didn't blink an eye.

'Forty-three,' Nick growled. 'I'm looking for Ms Drake.'

That, for some reason, did make the concierge blink. 'Ms Drake?'

Nick was a patient man, but not today. He saw no point in repeating something that had been perfectly clear in the first place. He watched the hand crawl from five to four.

'You won't find Ms Drake,' said the concierge, and there was something in his voice that made Nick look away from the dial and at him again. His thin lips were pursed, his blue eyes practically bugging out of his head. If Nick didn't know better, he'd think the little glaring guy was close to tears.

The elevator dinged. 'I'll wait,' Nick said, pulled the grille aside, and stepped into the elevator.

'You'll be waiting a while,' the concierge said, but Nick pressed the button for the fourth floor and the doors were closing.

Over two hours later, Nick had to admit the concierge had been right. Irritatingly right. Nick rubbed his hand over eyes that felt as if they were full of sand and considered his options.

He could stay in this corridor easily for several days, as far as food and drink were concerned. But unless he used one of his water bottles, he was going to need a break soon. He very much doubted that the concierge would direct him to a restroom in the building, and it would be just his luck if his quarry returned while he was searching Manhattan for a public convenience.

Nick closed his eyes. He wasn't going anywhere. He was sticking it out. He was good at waiting. He'd waited sixteen years for this day, after all.

If only that damned clock would stop ticking.

The elevator dinged and Nick opened his eyes. Without moving from his position on the floor outside apartment forty-three, he turned his head towards the elevator.

If a man stepped out, would Nick even recognise him? Were his memories that clear? What would have changed in sixteen years?

The bronze grille slid open and a woman stepped out into the corridor and headed his way. The feeling in his stomach was, strangely, like both disappointment and relief. He watched her approach.

She was medium height, in her twenties, with blonde hair in a short style tucked behind her ears. Within a split second Nick could tell she wasn't Ms Drake. He didn't know much about Ms Drake, but knew she used heavy, high-quality writing paper, expensively embossed with her return address, which was a corner apartment of one of the most exclusive buildings in the upper west side of Manhattan. Ms Drake did not wear a huge ill-fitting ancient black leather jacket, a black skirt even Nick could tell was out of fashion, and battered running shoes.

Probably a cleaner or a nanny or something. Nick began to look away, but the blonde caught his eye with her own. She nodded a slight greeting, her chin high, her broad mouth unsmiling.

Nick nodded back and shifted his gaze to the tasteful wall across from him. No point antagonising the neighbours' hired help.

'Looks like you could do with a cushion,' she said. Her voice was surprisingly low and throaty.

'I'm okay. It's a lot more comfortable than the top of a mountain,' he replied, and exchanged half a smile with her before dropping his gaze again.

'The view's not as good, though.' She walked past him, giving his hiking boots a wide berth. Though her skirt was ugly, her bare calves and ankles were well toned and defined. She was no gorgeous Manhattan socialite, but she did have good legs.

'It's not too bad,' he said.

She chuckled and he heard keys jingle. Nick looked up sharply to see her inserting a key into the door to apartment forty-three.

In an instant he was on his feet. 'Ms Drake?'

She tilted her head up towards him, her slight smile disappearing from her lips, and slid the key out of the lock. 'Yeah?'

It was impossible to tell her size with that jacket on, but she suddenly drew herself up taller and when Nick glanced down he saw that she had her keys between her fingers, held stiff as if to serve for a weapon.

New York, what a hell of a town, Nick thought, and eased back so as to appear less aggressive. Not an easy thing to do while his heart was beating a mile a minute and his entire body was tense.

'My name is Nicholas Giroux,' he said.

'Uh huh.' Her blue eyes, narrowed before, relaxed a little, but he couldn't see any recognition in them.

'I'm Eric Giroux's son.'

The blonde looked him up and down, and then one of her eyebrows lifted and the corner of her mouth came up, too. 'Well, that's nice for you,' she said. 'Excuse me, I'd like to go inside now.' She turned to the door and slid the key back into the lock.

She was mocking him. Fine. Nick didn't care. What this woman thought wasn't important. All he wanted was what she knew.

He stepped closer to her. He kept his face calm and his eyes steady on hers, as he would when showing a dangerous animal who was boss. The woman stood unmoving, her hand on the doorknob, her bottom lip and her chin thrust out, her own eyes defying his stare.

'Where is my father?' he demanded.

There was a tall, dark, handsome, very angry man on the doorstep. Well. And she'd thought today couldn't get any weirder.

Zoe stood poised with her hand on the doorknob, equally

ready for fight or flight. She didn't need to size the guy up; she'd done it already, when she'd first seen him lounging against the wall in the corridor. He was about six two, probably two hundred pounds and all of it muscle. His hands looked big enough to crush her skull like a bug. And he was fast.

She thought she could probably take him.

Then again, by all indications he was insane, and insane people were harder to beat.

'I don't know where your father is,' she said pleasantly. 'Do you lose him often?'

'Very funny,' said the man, but he wasn't laughing. Just as well. When he'd smiled at her earlier he'd been even more gorgeous, and she really didn't need the distraction, what with him possibly being some sort of mental psycho killer with a father fixation.

She continued in the same cheerful tone, 'I'm sorry I can't help you. You know sometimes when I lose something I go back to the last place I saw it and work forward from there. I'm not sure it works with lost people, though.'

He clenched his teeth, making his jaw seem even stronger, took another half-step towards her, and Zoe knew that while he'd been mad before, now he was furious.

She'd dealt with quite a few aggressive people. There were lots of scumbags in New York, and most of them seemed to cross her path at some time or other. This guy wasn't one of them. His dark brown eyes were narrowed and flashing; his well-formed mouth was compressed. But he wasn't going to hurt her.

She could see it in the restraint of his shoulders and the humour lines beside his mouth. He was strong, but he wasn't violent. And she'd bet he didn't get angry very often, either.

She'd been calm up till now—well, as calm as she could be, given her errand to her great-aunt's apartment. But with that re-alisation, her pulse sped up.

He was tall, dark, handsome, self-controlled, and on some sort of quest. Just her freaking type.

This guy might not be dangerous in general. But he was dangerous to her.

'Listen,' he said, 'I've waited a long time and I've come a long way to find my father.' His words were carefully paced. 'You can laugh all you want, but I'm going to find him.'

'Hey, I'm not laughing. Good luck. I hope you find your dad if it means that much to you.' She twisted the doorknob. 'Well, it was nice meeting you but I've had one hell of a day and I've got to do something I'm not looking forward to.'

His hand unclenched and dropped over hers on the doorknob. Zoe's throat closed up. His palm was warm and his fingers strong. A charge of desire zapped through her body.

Oh, damn.

'Your name is Drake, right?' His voice had sunk to low intimacy, still angry, but controlled.

She tried to answer and couldn't. All of her brains had migrated between her legs. This was a dangerous, dangerous man. She nodded.

He leaned even closer to her, so close she was breathing his scent. He smelled like outdoors. Leaves and living earth. His eyes were incredibly dark and he hadn't shaved for a couple of days. Nor, she would bet, had he slept. Up close his face was weary.

'Ms Drake, you don't have to cover for him. He wrote to me. That means he wants me to find him. Just let me in, and let me talk to him.'

Let me in. He meant into the apartment. Zoe was coming up with entirely different interpretations, which involved letting him into her body, into her mind, into her life.

'You think your father is in this apartment?' Zoe asked.

'Yes.'

Well, that was a point. For all she knew, he might be. For all she knew, the whole New York Giants football team might be in there. She hadn't been to her great-aunt Xenia's place for a few weeks.

'Have you knocked?' she asked.

'Nobody answered,' he said. 'That was why I was waiting for you.'

'So…you think there might be a man waiting inside this apartment who's not answering the door?' That thought was a little creepy. Quite a bit creepier than this guy waiting outside the apartment.

'That's why I want to go in.'

'Listen,' she started, squaring her shoulders and firming her resolve, 'I really don't—'

'Please.'

The word was full of longing and of loss. Zoe stared at his dark eyes, no longer narrowed but open and full of feeling. This man, Nicholas he'd said his name was, missed his father. He wanted him back.

Even though it was probably for two totally different reasons, and certainly for two totally different people, right now, she and this man shared exactly the same emotion.

Suddenly, fiercely, Zoe wanted her great-aunt Xenia back. And Xenia was gone for ever.

She twisted the doorknob under his hand and pushed the door open. 'Go ahead,' she said. 'Have a look.'

He dropped her hand and went past her into the apartment.

'Manners,' Zoe murmured, watching him rush past her. But she couldn't take much offence; the guy was in a hurry and she was the last person on his mind. He'd even left his enormous backpack in the hallway. And if there was somebody skulking in here, she could use some backup.

Hold on. Backup? Three minutes ago she'd thought this guy was a psycho killer and now she was thinking of him as backup?

Zoe shrugged. Stranger things had happened to her today already, and at least this was a good distraction from why she was really at the apartment. She followed him inside, closing the door behind her.

He was halfway down the entrance hall already, giving her the opportunity to observe that he was also good-looking from behind: broad-shouldered and narrow-waisted. A great butt. His brown hair curled slightly on the back of his neck. When she got to the living room she leaned against the doorway and watched him looking around.

It was a big room, with floor-to-ceiling windows and enough

furniture and screens to make it not immediately obvious that there wasn't anybody else in it except for the two of them. The man scoped it out with quick efficiency, looking swiftly in the reading nook behind the Chinese silk screen, behind the tall arm-chairs and into the corners and even, briefly, behind the heavy velvet drapes.

Zoe saw with amusement that for all his searching he didn't seem to notice the collection of thumbscrews on the wall or the chain-saw in the glass case on a sideboard.

'Does your father usually lurk behind drapes?'

He didn't even spare a glance for her; instead he opened the door to the library. Zoe wandered across and watched him examine this room, too, and the study beyond it. She followed him back into the corridor, waited as he searched the big tiled kitchen, and then trailed after him as he headed towards the bedrooms.

'If you tell me what your dad looks like I'll help you,' she said.

'About six feet tall,' he said, not glancing at her as he opened a closet door and then closed it again. 'Brown hair, brown eyes, forty-eight years old.'

'You mean he looks like you, except older.' Zoe pretended to consider. 'And he's fond of hiding in closets, apparently.'

Nicholas turned, walked towards her, stopped, crossed his arms on his impressive chest, and looked at her. He started at the top of her head and took her in, head to toe, with a flash of his dark eyes. She noticed he didn't exactly linger on her body or her face.

The attraction was one-way, then. What a surprise.

'I don't have your father hidden underneath my clothing,' she said.

He didn't acknowledge the crack. 'I'm trying to figure out how far I trust you.'

'Hey, *you're* the one who was hanging outside in the corridor looking suspicious.'

'You're the one who has a chain saw in your living room.'

He had noticed, then. 'Well, a girl has to protect herself.' She smiled at him, though he didn't smile back. 'When was the last time you saw your father?'

'Sixteen years ago.'

'And what makes you think he's in this apartment?'

'Because this is his last known address.'

That made her blink, though it probably shouldn't. Her great-aunt Xenia must've had plenty of guests in her apartment. And some of them were bound to be male guests. Just because Xenia had never married didn't mean she didn't like male company, and if Nicholas's father was as attractive as Nicholas was, Zoe couldn't blame her great-aunt for letting him move in for a while.

'Is he your lover?' Nicholas Giroux asked.

That really did make her blink. 'What? Your *father*? No.'

Nicholas searched her face more closely. 'You're not his daughter, are you? Are we related?'

Zoe laughed. As if she and this god could possibly be related. 'My father is Michael Drake and he lives in Fairfield, New Jersey. I wouldn't mind losing him sometimes.'

'What's your connection to my father?'

'I don't have any. I told you I don't know him.'

'No, you didn't. You said you didn't know where he was.'

She thought back. He was right. 'Well, I don't know him, either.'

Nicholas shook his head, and even though she'd just met him, she could recognise exasperation. He turned his back on her and opened the door to the first bedroom.

This was Xenia's guest bedroom, the one that Zoe usually used when she stayed over, and Nicholas's conviction that he would find his father was so strong that Zoe almost expected to see an older version of Nicholas stretched out on the bed reading *Sports Illustrated*.

But the bed was made, the room empty.

He only had to glance into the second bedroom, which was full of junk and boxes and a small cot, and then he was twisting the knob of the third bedroom, Xenia's bedroom, which had been Zoe's destination in the first place.

'If you haven't seen your father in sixteen years, how do you know this was his last known address?' she asked, quickly, to distract him from opening the door. She didn't want to go into that bedroom; she didn't want to do what she'd come here to do. It would make the truth too real and too permanent.

Nicholas reached inside his coat. He was wearing a weatherproof jacket, as a hiker would wear. It went with his all-weather trousers and his waterproof boots. Nice that he had a style theme going, anyway: rugged outdoorsman, not a common look in New York City. Of course, the man would look delectable in a plastic sack.

He pulled out a crumpled, cream-coloured envelope, and Zoe recognised it right away. She'd received letters in envelopes like that, written on matching stationery, embossed with this address, on every birthday since she could read. Even though they were standing right in the middle of Xenia's apartment, the envelope was an almost shockingly intimate reminder of her great-aunt.

'Xenia knew him,' she said, almost to herself.

Nicholas had been extending the envelope to her, but he stopped mid-air. 'Xenia? Who's Xenia?'

'My great-aunt. She owns this apartment.'

Owned.

'*You* don't own this apartment?'

Zoe spread her hands out on either side of herself, indicating her big leather jacket, her worn-in running shoes, and her frankly gross skirt—all of them the only black clothes she happened to own that weren't skin-tight spandex.

'Do I look like I own this apartment?'

He raised his eyebrows and twisted the side of his mouth in an acknowledgement that was, even though she'd asked for it, a little too readily given for her ego. Yeah, she looked like a taste-less girl from the Bronx dumped in a classy Manhattan apart-ment. He didn't have to rub it in.

'Why did you say you owned this apartment?'

'I didn't,' she said, glad that this time she remembered the con-versation better than he did. 'I had a key for it and you assumed it was mine.'

'Why do you have a key for it?'

Ah, now that was the question.

'Xenia died three days ago,' she said. 'I was coming here to get clothes for her to be dressed in for her funeral. I got the call out of the blue this morning from the funeral director to say that she'd appointed me to arrange things for her.'

'Oh.' Right away, and seemingly without any conscious decision, his expression softened, from challenging to gentle. 'I'm sorry.'

Zoe got the sudden urge to step forward, press her face against the fabric of his jacket, and ask him to wrap those strong arms around her and give her a hug.

She couldn't remember the last time she'd had a hug. Or wanted one.

God, she must really be attracted to this guy if she was thinking of pathetic excuses to touch him.

She shrugged. 'Not your fault. At least it's been amusing to watch a total stranger ransacking my great-aunt's apartment.'

Nicholas inclined his head to the last unopened door. 'Is this her bedroom?' His voice was gentle as his expression.

Tall, dark, handsome, angry, and kind. Zoe plastered a grin onto her face and crossed her arms over her chest, where her heart was beating with a new crazy, stupid longing of its own.

'You think your dad's in there?'

'Only one way to find out,' the perfect stranger said, and he opened the bedroom door.

CHAPTER TWO

THE BED WAS vast, satin-covered, and empty. The rest of the bedroom, expensively furnished in cream and mahogany, silk-wallpapered, tasselled and mirrored, was equally empty. Zoe was relieved to see that it looked exactly the same as the last time she'd seen it. She didn't know what she'd been expecting: a sign on the bed saying 'Sorry, I'm Dead'?

No. She'd been expecting emptiness. But there wasn't any emptiness in this apartment; every single inch of it breathed with Xenia, even though Xenia was gone.

Maybe it took some time for an apartment to understand its owner was dead. When that owner was somebody like Xenia, full of life and adventure, it probably took even longer.

She noticed that Nicholas was standing beside her. He hadn't made any move to go into the bedroom.

'Don't you want to search the closet?' she asked him.

He stayed where he was, gazing into the room. 'Why does your great-aunt have a bear trap in her bedroom?'

The trap was on a table at the foot of her bed, in a glass case like the one that held the chain-saw in the living room. Its shiny, well-oiled jaws gaped open, as they had for years.

'Like I said, a girl needs to protect herself somehow.' She moved into the room, and when he didn't follow she looked back at him. His dark eyes were settled on her, and she felt a hot flush underneath her ugly clothes. If he made a move to touch her, there was no way she'd ever set the bear trap on him.

But he wasn't flirtatious, and what she saw was curiosity, not desire. She gave up the snarky answers and shrugged. 'Xenia's had it for a while. I don't know where it came from.'

He nodded and this time did come into the room. She noticed once again how he walked with an easy athleticism, a natural economy of movement. A guy like that would have stamina and patience, both in bed and out of it. Pity it wouldn't be with her.

'You said you needed to get some clothes for her?'

Zoe dragged her attention away from pointless speculation about what this guy would be like as a lover and focused herself on the task at hand. The sooner she got it over with, the sooner she wouldn't have to dread it. She marched herself over to her great-aunt's walk-in closet. Before she opened the door, she couldn't resist looking at Nicholas over her shoulder.

'I don't care if he's your father, if he leaps out of this closet I'm going to knee him in the crotch.'

Nicholas said something under his breath; it sounded like, 'Be my guest.' He had something against his dad, all right. Zoe opened the closet door.

She saw nothing but row after row of shoes and designer outfits. She stepped back from the door so that he could see in, too. 'Sorry, Nick, no luck, unless he's disguised as an evening gown.'

Nicholas nodded. 'Are you all right?' he asked.

Once again, his concern surprised her. This guy didn't know her from Eve and, from the sound of it, he had enough problems of his own. Surely he couldn't tell how her stomach was twisting with dread at the idea of having to go through her great-aunt's clothes and find exactly the outfit Xenia had specified in her funeral plan.

'Yeah, I'm great,' she said. 'Just disappointed I didn't get to work on my crotch-kicking skills.'

'I'm not going to offer to help you out there.'

'Pity.' She gave him a smile that should cover up any hint of what she was feeling—the dread, and most especially the fact that she was touched by his concern. 'Well, your dad's not around, so feel free to split if that's what you plan on doing.'

'I'm fine here,' he said. He leaned comfortably against one of the high mahogany bedposts, as if he lounged around in outdoor gear in fancy bedrooms every day of his life.

'I'll be done in a minute. You can wait in the living room if you want, or in the kitchen. You might as well go ahead and make yourself some coffee, you look like you need some.' *Xenia won't mind,* she was about to add, but then she caught herself.

'I'll stay here. You probably could use some company. It can't be easy going through her clothes.'

She didn't want to stare at him, but she did, because she didn't want this stranger's kindness but at the same time it felt amazingly, scarily good.

He gave her his gentle half smile.

Zoe shook herself. 'Whatever.' She turned her back on him and went into the closet.

The clothes smelled of Xenia's spicy, exotic perfume. Zoe breathed in and kept the air inside her lungs for as long as she could.

'Please bury me in my black Gaultier sequinned gown,' Xenia had written in her funeral plan, 'with the silver fox collar cloak and the black Vuitton shoes.' Zoe flipped through endless hangers, wondering how she was going to know the right gown when she saw it. Her great-aunt had millions of the damn things, and Zoe wouldn't know a Gaultier if the designer came up and slapped her in the face with a frock.

But she did remember this green jacket; it was what Xenia had been wearing the last time Zoe had seen her. She pushed it aside, firmed her lips into a thin line, and kept looking. She ignored the prickling in her eyes.

'So do you always let strange men into your apartment?'

She snapped her head up to see that Nick had come to the closet and was leaning against the doorpost. He had obviously perfected the art form of looking gorgeous while he was minding other people's business.

'I told you, it's not my apartment.'

'It's still a stupid thing to do. I could have been anybody.'

'You want me to practise my crotch-kicking skills after all?'

He held up his big hands in a placatory gesture. 'Just pointing out some safety tips.'

'And here's one for you: stop criticising me.'

She glared at him. He put his hand over his mouth, but his brown eyes still smiled at her. She turned her back on him and resumed her search.

It took her a couple of minutes and a dozen outfits before she realised her eyes weren't prickling any more.

She shot Nick another look, but his face was neutral, and it was impossible to tell if he'd been goading her on purpose to distract her. But she suspected he had.

Her hand landed on something soft and sleek; without looking she knew it was the cloak. It was made up of yards of soft black material, with a silver fur collar.

'Fox?' Nick said.

'Funny, I wouldn't have pegged you as an expert on fashion.' She pulled it off the rail.

'I'm not. I've seen pelts like that walking around.'

She shrugged. 'Bear traps, chain saws, fox fur. Xenia was lots of things, but politically correct was never one of them.'

The Gaultier dress was next to the cloak. Zoe took it off the rack. Even on the hanger it looked tiny; Xenia, like most of the Drake women, had been graceful and elegant and beautiful, even into her seventies. Traits that Zoe Drake had definitely not inherited.

'Were you close to your great-aunt?'

Carrying the clothes, Zoe brushed past Nick on her way out of the closet. She could actually feel the difference in scent, from the perfumed closet to Nick's breath of outdoors. She laid the clothes on the satin bedspread.

'Not really, not in the regular way. We didn't tell each other everything. I didn't really know her. She let me stay here when I needed somewhere.'

Why was she telling this to a stranger?

'I have no idea how I'm going to find her shoes,' she added. She turned back to the closet, doing her best not to see Nick's face.

'You loved her.'

She brushed past him again—big, tall, strong, annoying men took up a lot of space in doorways—and stooped to look at the array of shoes. Xenia had millions of dresses, but she apparently had sixty gazillion pairs of shoes, a good proportion of them black.

'Like I said. I didn't really know her.' She picked up some impossibly pointed heels, checked them for a label, put them back.

'That doesn't mean you didn't love her.'

Zoe's hand paused on a pair of pumps. She looked sharply up at Nick. His face was serious, far more serious than it would be if he were just talking about her.

Yeah. This carey-sharey stuff was so not her. 'Listen, I'm pretty sure there are a few kitchen cupboards you haven't checked yet for your father. You can go ahead and do that now. Otherwise, please shut up.'

He shrugged himself off the doorpost and joined her in the closet. The enormous walk-in closet was a hell of a lot smaller with him in it. And he was so...tempting.

He squatted down next to her.

'What are you looking for?'

'Shoes.'

'Yes, I gathered that. What kind of shoes?'

'I don't need help, thanks.'

He just stayed there next to her, big and still and warm. 'What kind of shoes?'

Zoe exhaled sharply. If she let him help her at least they'd get out of this closet more quickly and she wouldn't have to deal with her hormones. 'Black Vuitton heels.'

'What do black Vuitton heels look like?'

'Black. With heels.'

He surveyed the shoe racks. 'Every single one of these things looks like a recipe for a broken neck.'

'Tell me about it.' She looked at shoes, discarded them, and looked at some more.

'Then again, if you had good legs these shoes would look very sexy.'

The word went through her like a double shot of expensive whiskey, warming her from her throat to her toes.

He was speaking theoretically, of course. 'Maybe if you wear size fives.' She picked up a pair at random and saw the label: Louis Vuitton. They were black, and they had heels—extremely high and narrow ones, sharpening to a point at the end.

'What size do you wear?'

'Nine.' She stood, shoes in hand. 'Found them.'

Nick straightened himself up to his full height beside her. 'People walk in heels like that?'

'Fortunately, Xenia's not going to have to worry about that.' On her way out of the closet, she snagged a garment bag and immediately started packing up the clothes.

Nick emerged from the closet. 'Your great-aunt had interesting taste.'

'She was interesting in every way.'

'How do you think she knew my father?'

She let out a laugh. He was being kind to her, but he hadn't forgotten his own mission. 'I really have no idea, Nick.'

'What's your name?'

Zoe stopped zipping the garment bag. 'Why?'

'Because you know mine.'

She pulled the tab up to the top of the zipper, and knew another reason she should tell him her name. Because she'd just done the job she was dreading, and she hadn't shed a single tear.

Thanks to him.

'My name's Zoe Drake.'

'Hello, Zoe Drake.' Nick held out his hand, a cordial, winning smile on his perfect lips.

Well. Hadn't he been well brought up. Zoe gripped his hand with her own. For a moment her strength met his strength and for her at least it was a testing, as well as a greeting. He was firm and gentle and warm.

She dropped his hand. 'I'm done here. Coffee?'

He grimaced slightly. 'Actually I could really do with using the bathroom. I was waiting in that hallway for a long time, and I was beginning to think about using one of my water bottles.'

She laughed. 'Go ahead,' she said, and then glanced at Xenia's *en suite* bathroom. Zoe had never used it herself.

Before she could say anything Nick was already heading for the door out of the bedroom and into the hallway. 'I remember where it is, one up from the kitchen.'

Zoe followed him into the hall and watched him go into the guest bathroom, relieved that he had the good sense to know that using Xenia's bathroom would be too much of an intrusion. Not that it should matter, now—but it did.

She hung up the garment bag on a hook near the front door and found a tote bag to put the shoes in, and then she shucked her leather jacket and went into the kitchen. She never made coffee at home—why make it when the Greek deli next door made it better?—but she was used to the routine at Xenia's, because one of her jobs whenever she'd stayed over had been to make the coffee in the morning and bring it to Xenia in bed.

She found the beans in the freezer, otherwise empty except for ice trays, got out the grinder, measured the beans and listened to the familiar rattling buzz as the grinder did its work. She emptied it into the filter and added bottled water to the machine and sat at the table as the aroma of coffee filled the kitchen.

By all rights, this should be a sad thing to do. There was no Xenia to pour the coffee for. Zoe should feel lonely and mournful.

And yet it was as if by banishing her rare tears in the closet Nick had dulled the edge of her sadness. She'd been dreading finding Xenia's clothes, and yet he'd made her laugh.

Zoe frowned. What was she thinking? Not five minutes after she'd met him this guy had muscled into her great-aunt's apartment, and then just as quickly he'd muscled into her private life. And she was feeling all glad about it?

She stood and got down two mugs. She'd give him a cup of coffee, and then, father or no father, she'd kick his handsome butt out of here before she got even stupider.

* * *

Nick washed his hands and face in the marble sink and dried them on the fluffy white towel. After ten hours of driving and a couple more hours of waiting in a corridor, hot water and soap felt great.

He'd checked already, but he surveyed the bathroom once more for signs of male toiletries, some sign that his father had maybe stayed here. But the soap was scented and the shampoo was floral. There was a toothbrush in the medicine cabinet, but it was bright pink.

Nick remembered Eric Giroux as a big man, an outdoorsman, a hunter and a fisherman who always wore flannel and faded denim. It wasn't beyond the realms of possibility that Eric could use a pink toothbrush, but in itself it wasn't convincing evidence.

He'd only been able to cast a swift glance into the *en suite* bathroom, but he hadn't seen anything promising there, either. The most promising thing he'd seen in the whole apartment had been the bear trap, and even that was pretty ambiguous. He had no idea whether his father had hunted bear or not, and he was pretty sure if his father did hunt bear, he wouldn't keep his traps in glass cases.

Maybe later Nick would be able to do a real search. On the other hand, maybe later his father would come strolling through the door.

The scent of fresh coffee greeted Nick as soon as he stepped into the hallway; he followed it to the kitchen where Zoe sat at the table with two mugs in front of her. 'There isn't any milk,' she said. 'Xenia doesn't take it.' She frowned slightly. 'Didn't.'

'That's fine, I like it black.' Nick took the chair across from Zoe, and a sip of coffee. He leaned back with the mug warming his hand.

She'd taken off her leather jacket, revealing a black T-shirt that allowed him for the first time to see her shape. She was well built, with full breasts and a flat stomach and toned arms.

Nick's appreciation of this woman climbed a couple of points up the scale. She wasn't pretty—not like the women he was attracted to. Nick liked the small, feminine type, and Zoe wasn't delicate or overtly feminine: her jaw was too square, her mouth too wide, her nose too definite, her hands short-nailed and competent. But she was better-looking than he'd thought when he'd first seen her in the corridor. Especially when she was talking. Her mouth and eyes were mobile and interesting, and her movements were fluid. And her smile was bright and sudden.

She wasn't smiling now, though. She had her brows drawn down and her jaw was set. Her eyes were focused somewhere in the middle of the table.

'What's the matter?'

She glanced up at his face. 'Oh, only the obvious. I've got a funeral to arrange and there's this random guy barging into the apartment looking for his father.'

She was annoyed. Nick didn't mind that; he'd rather she was annoyed at him than sad about her great-aunt.

'Oh, that's all right. For a minute I thought you might be mad at me.' He took a leisurely sip of his coffee and watched her frown deepen. 'So, Zoe, what do you think? Did your great-aunt ever mention my father? Do you think he might be staying here still?'

Her blue eyes glinted at him. 'You really have a one-track mind, did you know that?'

'When I was ten years old, my dad went for a hunting trip one weekend and never came back,' he told her. 'My mother thought there had been an accident. She was frantic. I remember me and my sister going to school and trying to pretend that everything was all right, while my mother was at home, waiting. Two days after my father was supposed to be home, she got a phone call. I remember I was watching Bugs Bunny on TV when the phone rang.'

Zoe was still frowning, but her mouth had softened. 'What was it?'

'My mother thought it was the police calling to say my father was dead. I have never seen her so terrified, not before or since.'

Just retelling the story, Nick could feel the fierce protective instinct that had made him, at ten years old, turn off his cartoons and go to his mother and take her hand. His teeth had gritted against each other, his small body had drawn itself to its full height.

It was the moment he had become a man.

'Nick?' Zoe had put her coffee down and was leaning forward

on the table. Nick realised he must have stopped speaking, caught up in memory.

'It was my dad on the phone. I could recognise his voice through the receiver, so I knew it was him. I couldn't hear what he said, though. When my mother put the phone down she told me that my father hadn't been hurt hunting, he was fine, but he'd gone away and we wouldn't be seeing him for a while. About a month later she packed up his stuff and put it in the attic.'

'And you didn't hear anything from him at all until this letter?'

'I think my mom got envelopes with money in them occasionally, but not often, and not much. And she'd never show me the return address. She burned the envelopes before I could get my hands on them. I think she knew I'd go off to find him.'

'Looks like she was right.'

'My mother is usually right. I was too young then. The envelopes stopped when I was sixteen.'

'Were you afraid he was dead?'

'If he were dead he would have an excuse.'

He felt a pain in his hands and looked down at them to see them fisted, his knuckles white and the fingers red.

He swallowed and, after he had concentrated on his hands, they relaxed. He heard the kitchen clock ticking to the same artificial rhythm as the clock in the corridor outside. And, for a few seconds, he heard nothing else.

Zoe cleared her throat loudly. 'Well.' She pushed her chair back with a noisy scrape. 'It's been great talking about this, Nick, and thank you for sharing, but I've got to get home and do stuff, and I'm sure you're eager to comb the entire city for your missing father. Are you done with your coffee?' She held out her hand for his mug.

Nick didn't move. He flexed his hands and looked at the palms. On each of them there were four red crescents where his short nails had dug into the skin.

'I'm not going anywhere,' he said calmly. 'I'm staying here.'

CHAPTER THREE

'YOU'RE WHAT?'

Zoe stared at Nick. He was tall and dark and handsome as ever with the added bonus of being principled, wounded, and passionate.

No, no, no. He ticked all her 'perfect man' boxes exactly. She could not have somebody like this around. She needed to get rid of him.

He rubbed his palms against his thighs. 'I'm staying here. Do you know for sure my father isn't living here?'

'Did you see any sign of him?'

'Nothing definite, but that doesn't mean anything. Do you know for a fact that your great-aunt didn't have anybody staying with her?'

'She never did when I stayed here.'

'And when was the last time you stayed here?'

'I stayed a night about five weeks ago.' She'd done a double shift and taught a late class and she'd been too tired to go all the way across town to her own apartment. She'd called Xenia and Xenia had left keys with the concierge, Ralph. Xenia had been in bed by the time Zoe had dragged her weary carcass into the apartment. Zoe hadn't woken her up.

She would have if she'd known it was one of the few times they had left.

'The letter I got from my father was dated eight days ago,' Nick said. 'April twenty-third.'

'You waited eight days before you camped outside Xenia's door? You're not as obsessed as I thought.'

'I only got it yesterday when I got home. I was on an island off the coast of Maine monitoring bird populations when it arrived.'

His voice was maddeningly calm. Zoe considered bending over and trying to pick him up and toss him out the front door. He had about eighty pounds on her. The best scenario was he didn't struggle and she only slipped the one disc in her back. The worst scenario was they ended up wrestling on the kitchen floor and she turned into a big wobbling Jell-O of lust while he laughed at her.

Instead, she pushed her hair behind her ears. 'Uh-huh. So you're trying to say he could've moved in since I was last here. Fair enough. But your dad isn't here, and Xenia is dead. So you might as well follow up some other lead.'

'I don't have any other leads. As far as I'm concerned, he might have gone out an hour ago to get some milk and a paper. I'm waiting for him.'

Once again he folded his arms on his chest. Then he settled himself back in his chair, stretching his legs out in front of him as if he were never going to move.

'But I've got stuff to do,' Zoe said. 'I need to go home.'

'So go home. That's fine.'

'I can't go home and leave you here alone!'

'You think I'll get lonely? That's very kind of you. But I spend a lot of time alone, you don't have to worry about me.'

Zoe banged her hand against her thigh. 'No! I mean, I can't leave you alone in Xenia's apartment. I don't know you.'

'You trusted me enough to let me in.'

'Yeah, but that was—'

What had that been? From the looks of the immovable Nick and his big old easygoing smile, it had been a pretty colossal mistake.

'I can't leave you here,' she repeated.

'So stay. That's fine with me, too.'

'But—' Agh! Didn't this guy listen to reason? 'I need to get Xenia's clothes to the funeral parlour.'

Nick raised his eyebrows. 'Zoe, tell me if I'm being rude here—'

'You are,' she interrupted, but he continued straight on.

'But your great-aunt Xenia owned an enormous apartment in one of the most expensive areas of New York. I'm betting her funeral isn't going to be a low-budget affair.'

Zoe remembered the instructions she'd read this afternoon, written by her great-aunt in her funeral plan: the mid-Manhattan church to reserve, the private hotel ballroom to book, the request for vintage champagne and single-malt whiskey at the wake. 'What difference does that make?'

Without needing to leave his chair, Nick reached over and took the kitchen phone off its hook on the wall. He held it out to her. 'The difference is the funeral parlour is going to be paid a lot. They'll send someone over to pick up the clothes.'

She shook her head. 'Nick, I don't want to stay here. I don't live here. All my clothes are in the Bronx. Why don't you just—?'

'Zoe, I'm not going. I'm sorry that it's inconvenient for you, but this is my one chance.'

She grabbed the phone from his hand. 'Fine. I'll call the police.'

'Funny,' he said softly. 'I wouldn't have thought you needed someone else to fight your battles for you.'

It was as if he'd poked a crafty finger just exactly in the right place. Zoe winced.

'The only thing that matters to me is finding my father,' Nick said. 'I'll do whatever it takes. I really am sorry if it makes your life difficult. But it's made my life difficult for the past sixteen years. I can't leave without some answers.'

He held her eyes steady with his own. He looked big and immovable and very serious.

The doorbell rang.

Nick and Zoe's gazes flickered in the direction of the door, and then met again.

'Are you expecting anybody?' he asked quietly.

'I have no idea.'

He rose to his feet. Without a word, they fell into step across the kitchen and down the corridor to the front door. Nick was slightly ahead and he reached his hand out to the doorknob.

'No,' Zoe said, and he stopped. 'It's my great-aunt's apartment,' she explained to his enquiring look. For a moment she didn't think he was going to back down, but then he nodded and stepped back.

Zoe reached her hand towards the doorknob and realised she was holding her breath.

Up until this moment, she hadn't really believed that Nick's father was hanging around Xenia's apartment. Sure, there was plenty she didn't know about her great-aunt's life—most everything, actually—and anything was possible with Xenia, but it hadn't seemed quite right. Xenia had been so independent, so in love with her own way, so much like Zoe, in fact, that Zoe couldn't picture her sharing her space with anybody.

But Nick was standing as if he were expecting an explosion. Every fibre of his body was tense; she could feel it even with the couple of feet of air between them. She heard his breathing coming in shallow, quick bursts. She had the feeling that if she edged a little closer to him, she would be able to hear his heart beating.

He wanted his father to turn up so badly that she couldn't help wanting it, too.

'Will you know him?' she asked softly.

'I don't know.'

She looked at his face. There were lines around his eyes and mouth: tension and hope and, she thought, fear.

Zoe turned her attention to the door, twisted the knob, and stared at the man standing outside.

Geez, he's short for Nick's dad, she thought, and then she saw it was Ralph, the concierge.

He looked almost as surprised to see her as she was to see him. Zoe found her voice first.

'Hey, Ralph, how's it going?'

'Zoe.' He swallowed, most definitely at a loss for words, which was unusual because normally he was a nosy son of a gun. 'I didn't see you come up.'

'You were out back, I think, when I came in. I didn't bother you because I had my own set of keys.' And because she hadn't felt like exchanging sympathetic after-death chat with him, or anybody. She'd hovered outside the front door of the building until she'd seen him turning his back on the desk to fill his ever-present coffee mug, and then she'd dashed through the door and run to the elevators as quickly as she could.

'Oh. Well I was just checking—there was this guy who said he was looking for Ms Drake—'

Nick stepped behind her, into Ralph's line of sight. Zoe felt his warmth on her back and breathed his scent suddenly surrounding her, as intimate as a hug.

'I found her,' he said.

Ralph looked taken aback. 'Oh—I, er, thought you meant—'

'He did,' Zoe said. 'But since my great-aunt has died he decided I would do just as well.'

Ralph's eyes narrowed, looking between them. Although Zoe had known Ralph for years, she felt all at once as if he were suspecting her of planning to rob Xenia's home. 'And you're both all right? Can I help you with anything?'

'Fine,' Zoe said firmly. 'Thank you, Ralph.'

She began to close the door, but his hand shot out and stopped her. 'It's just that his backpack is still in the hallway, so I wondered—' he lowered his voice, and spoke close to Zoe's face '—if you had invited him in yourself.'

Zoe didn't know what he was being protective of—her welfare, or Xenia's belongings. Either way, habit and instinct chose her next words for her.

'I only do what I want to do, Ralph. And I'm doing fine. Thanks so much for your concern, though.'

Behind her, Nick spoke. 'And thanks for reminding me about my pack.' He brushed past her into the hallway.

For a split second the length of his hard, warm body was pressed against hers and Zoe's awareness filled with a huge, hopeless longing. She was barely able to understand how her stomach was twisting, her nipples hardening, her legs weakening, before he had swept the big backpack up without any effort and had brushed past her again, back into the apartment.

This time he pressed even closer against her, because the pack took up extra room. Her hip brushed his groin and the back of his arm touched the side of her right breast.

Zoe's lips parted, her body throbbed, and she nearly moaned with the pleasure from that contact, unintentional and unavoidable as it was. For a stunning moment she knew that if he really touched her, naked skin on naked skin, touched her with desire in his hands, it would be beyond anything she had ever felt before.

And then she shut her mouth as she realised what had just happened.

Uh, der, Zoe! Stupid girl! Nick had just left her apartment and she'd been too busy dealing with hormones to shut the door behind him.

She'd had backup, too. Ralph was still in the hallway, looking suspicious. If she'd really wanted to get rid of Nick, she would have asked him for help, and damn her independence.

But she hadn't.

'See ya, Ralph,' she said, and shut the door.

Nick had already gone down the hall and into the living room. When she got there he was sitting on the couch checking over his backpack. It was a very big backpack, cared-for but well worn.

'So do you travel with your life on your back or what?' she asked. She considered sitting in an armchair safely across the room from his sexy body, but Zoe had never been one to go for the safe option. Her actions just now proved it. She dropped onto the couch beside him.

'Just like a turtle,' he agreed. He unzipped the top and pulled out a charcoal-grey sweater, and then he pulled off his weather-proof jacket.

He was wearing a white T-shirt that clung to his wide shoulders and his muscular chest. His arms were well developed and tanned. Zoe's mouth went dry and she swallowed.

'I didn't know how long I'd be away for, so I thought it was

best to be prepared.' Nick didn't seem to notice that she was
making googly eyes at his chest.

'You'd make a good Boy Scout,' she said, not really paying
attention to what she was saying because he was rolling up his
jacket and putting it in his backpack and the movement made
the sinews and muscles of his arms flex in all sorts of wonderful ways.

'I was a great Boy Scout,' Nick said. 'Made Eagle Scout.
How about you—were you ever a Girl Scout?'

Zoe glanced down to see her nipples were hard and highly
visible underneath her own t-shirt. She forced her eyes away from
his chest before her lust became far too obvious.

'I'm not a joiner. My mother forced me to go to one Brownie
meeting with my older sister Jade and I deliberately poured milk
down the jumper of the head Brownie person.'

Nick laughed and his laugh was just as appealing as his
chest, warm and deep. Zoe curled herself into a corner of the
couch, wrapping her arms around her legs to keep herself in
control. 'So what else do you have in that backpack? A tent?
Cooking stove?'

'Yes,' said Nick, and she risked a glance to his face to see if
he was serious. He was.

'What were you going to do? Camp out in Central Park?'

'It occurred to me.'

Zoe snorted. 'Well, that's fine, then. You don't need to stay
here. You can go camp out in the park and I'll just open the
window and call you if your dad shows up.'

'Nope,' Nick said serenely. 'Staying here. Why are you so hot
to get rid of me, anyway?'

'I don't know you from Adam and as far as I can tell that
backpack is full of knives so you can cut me into little pieces and
then steal all my great-aunt's valuables.'

Good thing she was such a good liar, because there was no
way she was going to tell him the real reason she didn't want him
to stay—that she was afraid if she spent much more time with
him she'd get to like him.

Then again, that could be a pretty good way of getting him to leave. He'd think she was the biggest freak in the universe, which, come to think of it, could be true.

'Well, I tried to point out earlier that I might be dangerous, and you told me to shut up.' He opened a different compartment of his backpack and began to rummage inside it.

'Besides,' she said, 'I have other places to be.'

'Oh.' He looked up from his backpack. 'Do you have a date or something?'

The appropriate response to that was to fall on the floor laughing. Zoe Drake, with a date on a Sunday night? She managed to control herself. 'I work a lot of evenings.'

'Do you need to work tonight?'

'No,' she admitted.

'That's good. I could do with the company. Besides your friend Ralph and some toll booth workers on I-95 on my way down here, I haven't spoken to another human being face to face for a week and a half.' He smiled at her and his teeth were straight and white and she felt like melting.

'And this fact is supposed to make me feel more reassured that you're not a psycho?'

'I'm not a psycho.' Nick held out something wrapped in a silver foil pouch. 'Do you want something to eat?'

As soon as he asked the question Zoe felt her stomach grumble. She was absolutely starving. She'd worked a nine-hour shift from six this morning on not much more than a ham sandwich, and then she'd gone for a run to clear her head and then gone to the funeral parlour.

'What is it?' she asked.

'A protein bar.'

She made a face. 'I'm hungry, but not hungry enough to eat that.'

He shrugged and peeled back the wrapper. 'You're welcome to anything else I've got.' He took a bite of the bar and, although it smelled unappetising even at this distance, her stomach rumbled again.

'What else have you got?'

'Dehydrated soup, some vacuum-packed stew and pasta, trail mix, a whole bunch of nuts.'

'How'd you grow so big on a diet like that?'

He laughed. 'I left in a hurry and took what I had left over from my two weeks on Cranberry Island. I'm actually a pretty good cook on a camp stove, when I can get the right ingredients. Do you think there's anything in your great-aunt's kitchen?'

'No. Xenia never cooked. I'll tell you what there is, though.' Zoe jumped up from the couch and went to a side table, where she picked up the cordless phone and a sheaf of take-out menus. 'We have a whole world of food at our fingertips. We only have to pick a country and a style. Chinese, Italian, Turkish, Indian, Japanese, American?'

Nick crumpled up the wrapper of his gross protein bar. 'I haven't had a pizza in weeks.'

'Now, that's one number Xenia doesn't have. She never ate anything bigger than an oyster with her hands.' Zoe began to dial. 'Fortunately, I have the number memorised. Pepperoni?'

'With mushrooms. And it's on me, so get an extra large.'

'If it's on you, I'll get two.' She dialled and ordered and put down the phone, realising she was resigned to spending the night with Nick in the apartment.

Well, if it was inevitable she might as well enjoy it.

Just not too much.

Nick swirled the dark red liquid around his glass thoughtfully. 'This is good wine, huh?'

'Too good to go with pizza, most likely.' Zoe took a swig from her glass and then took the last slice of pizza from the box without asking him.

She ate more than just about any woman he'd ever known, and she didn't preface every bite with worries about calories or vows to go on a diet the next day. She just ate it, with appreciation.

He'd grown up with two women, his mother and his sister, and he'd always been amused by the way they and most of the other women he knew treated food, as if it were their best friend and their worst enemy at once.

Zoe wasn't like that. For her, food was food, and if it tasted good, she liked it. She was like a guy that way. It was refreshing.

He took another sip of the wine Zoe had chosen from her great-aunt's extensive collection. It was dark and delicious, and it probably was fantastically expensive. Everything else in this apartment seemed to be. Even the chain-saw in the glass case next to the couch they sat on was a top model.

Working on and around Mount Desert Island, Maine's summer resort for the wealthy, Nick had met plenty of rich people. Zoe didn't fit that stereotype, either. It wasn't just because her clothes weren't fashionable; she was too down-to-earth for the rich type. Right now, for example, she was curled up on the end of the couch with her sock-clad feet on the cushion, licking pepperoni oil off her fingers.

Of course, just because her great-aunt was wealthy didn't mean Zoe had to be. She could've come from the poor side of the family.

'Where did your great-aunt get her money from?' he asked. In some company, it could be a rude question, but even from his short acquaintance with Zoe he knew she'd tell him to shut up if she didn't feel like answering. He found that refreshing, too.

She shrugged. 'I don't know. Nobody does.'

Nick raised his eyebrows. 'Nobody?'

'Well, she did, obviously, but I don't know anybody else who did. She didn't inherit it from a relative, because all of my ancestors were strictly middle-class. My parents used to speculate all the time. I think they were split between her inheriting it from an aristocratic lover, or her running a successful cathouse on the side.'

'A mistress or a madam?'

'My parents are often unnecessarily judgemental, they have very little imagination, and they have a hard time understanding life beyond their particular New Jersey suburb.' She folded up the remainder of the pizza slice and bit it in half. 'Personally I think it was something much more interesting.'

For the first time, she seemed to notice he had nothing left to eat, and she held out the folded-up pizza to him, a moon-shaped bite taken out of the end. 'Are you still hungry? Do you want any of this?'

Nick smiled. That was another thing that was refreshing about her—once she'd stopped trying to kick him out, she treated him as if she'd known him for years. 'No, thanks. What do you think she did?'

'Mostly, anything she wanted. I don't know how she got her money, but it must have been by some adventure or other. Xenia never stayed still for a minute.'

He heard pride in her voice instead of sadness. Good girl. She'd done well, too, when the guy from the funeral parlour had turned up just after the pizza-delivery man. For a minute she'd looked so sad, confronted by his black suit and sombre manner, that he'd thought she was about to cry. But she'd put on a smile and handed over the designer clothes without a blink, and then she'd gone and found a bottle of this expensive wine.

Though she acted differently, Zoe reminded Nick of his sister Kitty in some ways. After their father had left them, Kitty had cultivated the same skill of putting on a brave face. Kitty hadn't done such a good job of it.

Then again, Nick had already known what was going on underneath Kitty's brave face. Somehow he felt that Zoe wouldn't let him underneath her defences very easily.

'You want to be like Xenia, don't you?' he asked.

'I want to be like myself,' she replied, and immediately shoved the rest of the pizza in her mouth. Amused, he watched her chew. She definitely wasn't letting him underneath her defences.

'And what is yourself?' he asked. 'Are you fantastically rich, too?'

She swallowed. 'I drive a cab.' She took a drink of wine. 'And teach exercise classes.'

'Really?' He remembered the glimpse of her legs he'd had, and looked more closely at her arms. She was definitely fit, and she had that sureness of movement you found in people who used their muscles a lot.

'Really. And what about you? Do you get paid for counting birds on islands or is it just an eccentric hobby?'

'I get paid for it. I'm a park ranger.'

She put down her wineglass. 'A park ranger.'

'Yes.'

'Specialising in conservation, I bet.'

'Yes.'

'Principled,' she muttered. 'I knew it. Brother.'

'Excuse me?'

'Nothing.' She picked up her wineglass again and drank deep. 'A park ranger where?'

'Maine. I'm mostly based in Acadia National Park on Mount Desert Island, but I do some work on the outlying islands attached to the park, too.'

'A lone bird-counting ranger.' She polished off her wine. 'You must have to get back to the park pretty soon, huh?'

'I've got a week off. It isn't high season.'

'You're planning on staying here a week?' Her voice pitched up on the last word, probably, he thought, a result of the wine.

'It depends how long it takes to find my father. I can have more time off if I want it. I'm due some annual leave.'

'Aren't you worried that the Great Outdoors might perish without you to look after it?'

'Yes. But finding my father is more important.'

'Great. I'm trapped inside an apartment with a park ranger for a week.' Zoe reached for the bottle and splashed more wine into her glass.

'I'm hoping my father will turn up before then.'

'You're hoping he'll turn up tonight,' Zoe corrected. 'Well, I hope he does, too. What will you do if he doesn't?'

Nick picked up the bottle of wine. Zoe had taken the last of that, too.

'I'm not going to think about that possibility,' he said, and reached over. He took the glass of wine from her fingers, drank, and then held it back out to her.

She didn't take it. He looked at her face to see she was staring at him, her eyes wide, her generous mouth partly open. Her cheeks were flushed.

For a moment he thought he'd misjudged the situation, that he'd felt too comfortable with her, and that he'd forgotten himself and done something rude.

But she wasn't telling him off, and she wasn't looking annoyed. She was just…looking.

'Maybe I should finish this,' he said. 'You look like the wine's gone to your head.'

'Yeah,' she said. 'The wine.'

The words were slow and spoken softly. He saw her bite her bottom lip.

Then she closed her eyes and shook her head, as if she was deciding something with all of her will. She scooted to the edge of the couch and stood up.

'I think you're right. I think I should go to bed.'

She moved off, and her foot snagged on the rug in front of the couch. Nick saw it before she even started to fall, and in an instant he was up off the couch and catching her in his arms.

She was lighter than he'd expected and her body curved against his almost bonelessly. He'd been right; she'd had too much wine. She stared up into his face, obviously shocked from the fall.

'Nick—' she said, and even though she'd hardly tripped the shock must've been something, because her breath was coming in short pants, like that of a frightened animal. She leaned against him, being supported by him, but her hands dug almost painfully hard into his arms.

And the wine had gone to his head, too. Nick didn't drink much, usually, and he hadn't slept since he'd received the letter from his father yesterday. He felt his eyes slip out of focus and he felt a wave of fatigue form in his belly and make its way up and force his mouth open in a big, air-gulping yawn.

Zoe stiffened in his arms. She found her feet and pulled away from him.

'Okay, so I'm going to sleep in the spare bedroom, because that's where I always sleep,' she said, pushing her hair behind her ears and sounding not drunk at all, 'and you can have the boxroom, all right?'

'Actually I think I'll sleep in here on the couch. I've got a sleeping bag. I want to be close to the door in case my father comes in during the night.' He covered his mouth as another yawn overtook him.

'Suit yourself. Goodnight.' She picked up the pizza box and the wine bottle and left the room without a backwards glance. A minute later he heard her bedroom door shut, halfway across the big apartment.

Zoe lay in the dark, her eyes open and staring at the invisible ceiling. Her body was intensely awake.

She could blame the wine, but it was an excuse. It was her own fault. She'd been some kind of an imbecile to let herself relax, to let herself enjoy Nick's company, to sit so close to all that glorious, perfect, responsible maleness.

Idiot. She'd fooled herself into thinking it was going to be all right and that she wasn't going to fall for this guy and she could control her rampaging hormones and just share some pizza and wine. And then he'd reached for her glass, his fingers had brushed hers, he'd drunk her wine with a careless, sexy intimacy, and she'd known she was playing with fire.

Sixty seconds later she'd been in his arms and the desire had flamed through her like pain. Her knees had gone out from beneath her, her heart had thumped, her breath had stopped, her skin had leapt into excruciating life.

For a single dizzying, crazy moment, she'd thought maybe he was holding her because he was attracted to her, too. The possibility had made her swoon, like a silly girl.

She'd said his name in a breath of hope. And lifted her face for him to kiss her.

Then he'd yawned.

Zoe turned over and put the pillow over her head. She pressed her face into the warm sheet and wished she could bury herself there for ever.

The hell of it was, she could still feel his hands on her. He'd had one of them on her bare arm and the other on the small of her back. They burned into her, strong and deceptively safe-feeling.

At least she'd escaped before she'd tried to kiss him and made herself an object of pity.

At least.

Zoe turned back over and punched her pillow, hard.

CHAPTER FOUR

SOME PEOPLE FORGOT their problems in sleep. They woke up to blissful ignorance, and might even make it to their morning cup of coffee before they remembered what humiliating things they had done the night before.

Zoe had never had a moment of blissful ignorance in her life. Even before she opened her eyes she had one thought in her head: *I nearly threw myself at a guy who isn't the smallest bit interested in me.*

And the thought directly following that was: *I wonder if he still looks as beautiful this morning as he did last night.*

She shoved aside the blankets and climbed out of bed, pulling on her T-shirt and the ugly skirt. She had a toothbrush here at Xenia's but that was it; leaving actual clothes always seemed like too much to ask of Xenia, as if it was an intrusion on Xenia's independence. Now she wished she'd just left some, because Zoe hated skirts, and this one was itchy.

As soon as she opened the bedroom door she smelled coffee. Nick was up, then. On her barefoot way down the hall she resisted going into the bathroom and looking at her hair and face. The sight of her bedhead and her bleary eyes was not going to make her feel any better about herself, and Nick certainly didn't give a rat's ass what she looked like.

When she saw him leaning against the kitchen counter though, wearing jeans and a Red Sox T-shirt that hugged every inch of his perfect body, she nearly turned right back round to go and brush her teeth at least. But he spotted her first, and smiled.

'Sleep well?' he asked in that damn delectable voice and there was just enough mocking humour in it that she forgot about turning round and marched straight into the kitchen instead. The man was annoying and he could deal with her bad hair and her morning breath.

He made a move to take down a mug for her but she beat him to it and poured herself coffee without looking at him.

'A little hungover?' he said and she could hear the smile in his voice.

She made an elaborate act of peering around the kitchen. 'I don't see your father. Does this mean he didn't come sneaking into the apartment in the middle of the night after all?'

He shrugged. 'Maybe later. I'm not in a hurry. I've been waiting a long time to see him again.'

Zoe had her mug halfway to her mouth, but she slammed it down onto the counter, narrowly missing splashing coffee on her hand.

'Yeah, but did it occur to you that I might be in a hurry? I might want to get on with my normal life instead of playing baby-sitter to you while you make yourself at home in my dead great-aunt's apartment?'

Nick took a cloth from the sink and reached over to mop up the spill. Zoe snatched the cloth from him.

'Guess that answers my question,' he said. 'You're definitely hungover.'

'I wasn't drunk last night.' She scrubbed at the coffee harder than she needed to.

'If it's not a hangover, then what put the bug up your ass this morning?'

Being so attracted to you that I can't see straight when all you can do is comment on how rough I look. Zoe opened a cupboard, seeing only champagne glasses and yet more ice cube trays. 'There's no damn food in this apartment and I need breakfast.'

'I see. Low blood sugar makes you cranky. I've got a few more protein bars and that dehydrated stew in my backpack, if you want.'

Zoe pulled down a packet of something labelled 'Lapsang Souchong Tea'. 'I think I'd rather eat this,' she said, opening the top and recoiling at the pungent odour and sight of black leaves.

'What do you usually do for breakfast when you stay here?' Nick asked.

'I usually grab something from the deli down the block.'

'Well, let's do that.'

Zoe threw the cloth in the sink and took a frustrated swallow of coffee. 'We can't, remember? You don't want to leave in case your father shows up and in case I lock you out, and I don't want to leave in case you decide to steal all my great-aunt's antiques. We're at an impasse and we're both stuck here until you come to your senses and give up.'

'I'll go.'

Zoe stared. 'What?'

'I'll go to the deli and get us some breakfast. You can let me in when I come back.'

'But—what if your father turns up?'

'I'm sure you can keep him here for me.'

'But how do you know I'll let you back in?'

'I trust you.'

Zoe had been clutching her coffee-mug. She slowly set it down. Nick's dark eyes were steady on hers and, though he was smiling, he didn't appear to be laughing at her any more.

'Why?' she asked.

He shrugged. 'You're right, we're at an impasse. We have to trust each other sooner or later if we're going to get through it. Besides, even though you don't seem to believe my father had anything to do with your great-aunt, you know how important this is to me, and though you might be grumpy in the mornings I don't think you're the kind of person who would wilfully get in the way of somebody else's needs.'

'What makes you think that? I haven't exactly been overflowing with the milk of human kindness for you.'

'I see how you deal with your great-aunt's memory. You have respect. I think you respect my need to see my father.'

His smile had gone now and she saw, incredibly, that he was serious.

'Now that's something new. I've never been accused of being respectful before. Loud-mouthed and a pain in the neck, yes. Respectful and trustworthy, no.'

'There's a first time for everything, I guess.'

Zoe sat down and ran her hand through her tousled hair. 'I'll have a pumpernickel bagel with cream cheese and an orange juice.'

And his trust, apparently.

Nick nodded and threw her a smile and Zoe couldn't stop staring at the empty space he left after he was gone.

Maybe she had been a little hungover because after the bagel and a shampoo Zoe felt a hundred per cent better. She pulled on her ugly skirt again and went into the living room, where Nick was sitting on the couch next to his backpack. He'd evidently packed away his sleeping bag and all of his other stuff. He was looking contemplatively at the chain-saw in the glass case.

She took the armchair this time. He might trust her enough to leave the apartment, but she didn't trust herself enough to be close to him.

'So what's your plan for the day? Some more obsessive waiting for your father, maybe?'

'I'm wondering about the chain-saw and the bear trap,' Nick said. 'They don't seem like something that fits in New York City.'

'You think they could be connections to your dad?'

'Well, he had a chain-saw, but that's true of most people in Maine who burn wood for fuel. His wasn't as nice as this one—I know, because I was using it while I was still in junior high school.'

'He could have gone up in the world, I guess.'

'He only sent my mother twenty or thirty bucks at a time.' Nick's jaw set. 'But, yes, he could have.'

'Xenia's had the chain-saw for at least five years,' Zoe said. 'That would mean their connection wasn't very new, if it's his. But I wouldn't count on it. For all I know Xenia might have taken up chain-saw juggling.'

Nick's tense look turned into a smile. 'Your great-aunt would do that?'

'She died while skateboarding. She was seventy-four years old and she'd just started lessons.'

Nick laughed and, even though she'd been talking about Xenia's death, Zoe laughed, too.

'She'd have wanted to go that way,' she said. 'She fell and hit her head on the sidewalk when she was trying to ollie a four-set. Whatever that means. At the hospital they told me she never knew what hit her.'

'We had a retired ranger like that. On the morning of his eightieth birthday he climbed Cadillac Mountain. Got to the top, had a heart attack just as the sun climbed over the horizon. He was the first person in North America to see the sun rise and it was the last thing he ever saw.'

Nick stretched his long legs out in front of him and looked contemplatively at his boot-clad feet. 'If I could choose where I'd die, I'd choose Isle au Haut off the coast of Maine on a summer twilight. The day animals going to sleep, the night animals coming alive, and the moon rising over the Atlantic Ocean.'

The pleasure in his voice and on his face made Zoe able to picture the scene, even though he was describing it in a Manhattan apartment. It was about the third or fourth time he'd infected her with his thoughts and hopes, she realised.

'How about you?' he asked. 'Where would you want to go?'

In the middle of an orgasm with you buried deep inside me, panting my name into my ear, she thought, and then nearly smacked herself on the forehead.

Was there some sort of pill or lotion you could take for getting rid of lust?

'Oh, I'll take any old place as long as it's not in the gutter,' she said breezily. 'Though I've been in some pretty nice gutters over the years, too. Anyway, you never answered my question: what are you planning to do today?'

He didn't sit up, but he switched his contemplative look from his boots to her. 'The next logical step is searching your great-aunt's apartment for signs of him. Looking in her desk, her letters and bills for mentions of his name, things like that.'

Anger flushed up in her. And here she'd thought the guy had principles.

'No,' Zoe said immediately. 'Xenia was a private person. She didn't ask questions about me and I didn't ask questions about her. I'm not going to start going through her stuff just because she's dead. And if you think I'm going to let you, a stranger, paw through her private papers—'

'That's fine,' Nick interrupted.

Zoe stopped mid-flow. 'It's what?'

'It's fine. I understand how going through your great-aunt's stuff would be an invasion of her privacy. I'll have to find another way of finding out her connection to my dad.'

Zoe couldn't believe it.

'What about that whole "I'll do whatever it takes to find my father" line?'

'I guess I won't do whatever it takes. If I would, I would've gone through her study last night when you were asleep.'

She narrowed her eyes. Was he trying to tell her he'd done that very thing? And he wasn't putting up a fight now because he'd already found out what he needed?

And yet she remembered her instinct on the doorstep that he wouldn't harm her, angry as he was. The way he'd distracted her from sadness. How he'd floored her this morning with the three words 'I trust you'.

Life and the city had made Zoe suspicious. It only took one moment with your guard down to get it in the back, or worse.

But Nick was looking rueful, and he was rubbing his chin as if he felt foolish. Every instinct Zoe had was telling her this guy didn't have a false bone in his body.

'All right,' she said softly. 'Thank you.'

Nick nodded. 'Sure. So what are your plans today?'

'When I woke up, my plan was to sit here and stare you out until you got the hell out of the apartment. I was going to throw the cutlery at you, if necessary.'

'But things have changed,' Nick said.

'But things have changed,' she agreed. Though they had changed less than Nick probably thought. The revelation that he trusted her and that she trusted him meant it was even more urgent that she get rid of him as soon as she could.

And it looked as if the only way to do that was to help him find his father.

'I've got an appointment in half an hour to see Xenia's lawyer,' she said. 'He's going to go through the will. You should probably come along to see if it has any mention of your dad.'

Nick suddenly sat up straight. 'That's a great idea. Thanks.' He stood, unzipped his backpack, and pulled out a blue piece of clothing. Then he reached down and pulled his T-shirt up over his head.

Zoe gasped, and immediately snapped her mouth shut.

Nick's bare chest was spectacular.

In the split second before she turned her eyes away the sight of him was burned into her vision. He had broad shoulders and golden skin stretched over perfectly developed muscles. She could see and name them all: deltoids, pectorals, abdominals, obliques, every one of them defined and firm. A line of dark hair went from his navel downwards under the waistband of his jeans.

'God,' she muttered. She stared at the thumbscrews on the wall, thinking about torture.

'What is this, a strip show?' she managed to say at last.

'I thought I should put on nicer clothes if we're going to a lawyer's office,' Nick said, and she risked a glance. He'd put on the long-sleeved shirt and was buttoning it. Even through the cotton she could picture his naked chest.

She was probably going to picture it for the rest of her life.

Nick rolled up his T-shirt and shoved it back in the pack, and then pulled out a pair of dark trousers. Zoe jumped to her feet.

'I'll just make a phone call,' she choked, and fled the room before he decided to drop his jeans, too.

* * *

'How do you deal with all of this?'

Zoe dragged her attention away from the easy, sexy way Nick walked and glanced around her to see what he was talking about. The taxis beeped, the street vendors shouted, the homeless guy muttered, the sidewalk vents steamed. It was all normal.

'Deal with what?'

'Everything.' Nick swept his hands out in an all-inclusive gesture. 'The smell, for a start.'

Zoe sniffed in a deep breath and let it out. 'Hot dogs, concrete, gasoline, and somebody's perfume. What's wrong with that?'

'It's not air, it's fumes. Don't you feel like every breath is coating your lungs with gunk?' He grimaced.

'New Yorkers love gunk in their air.' She grinned at Nick and winked at him. He'd made himself so at home in her great-aunt's apartment, it was amusing to see him looking uncomfortable here on a New York street. 'Is the city too big for you, Eagle Scout?'

'It feels like another planet.' He pointed across the street, to the green trees and grass of Central Park. 'That, I understand. This, on the other hand—' he pointed right, towards the buildings '—is suffocating. All these walls. How do you ever feel like you're outdoors?'

'You know you're outside because the traffic gets louder. Come on, the office is up this block.'

They turned away from Central Park and Nick cast a longing look over his shoulder at the trees they were leaving behind. 'Were you born here?' he asked.

'Nope. In Jersey.'

'So you chose to move here.'

'The minute I turned eighteen.'

'Why?'

Zoe twisted the silver ring she wore on her thumb. She'd found it only a few blocks from here, kicked into a forgotten corner, and she wore it constantly to remind herself of everything else she'd found on the streets of New York.

'Because you can be yourself here,' she said. 'Nobody cares what you do.'

'That's appealing?' Nick manoeuvred around two men who were having a loud disagreement in a foreign language in the middle of the sidewalk. They carried on yelling at each other without taking any notice.

'Very.'

'But how can you feel as if you matter to other people, if everyone's so caught up in their own lives?'

'Why would you want to feel as if you mattered to other people?' She wasn't looking at him, but she felt Nick throw a sharp glance her way.

'Here's the lawyers' office,' she said, launching herself up the stone stairs before Nick asked any more questions. She wasn't sure how a general conversation about New York's pollution had turned into a big question-and-answer about her philosophy of life, but she had enough things to think about without it.

And two of those things were standing in the lobby waiting for the elevator up to the offices of Hopper, Stein and Feinberg, Attorneys-at-Law.

She padded up in her running shoes behind the two slim blondes and said, 'Yo, sis and sis.'

Jade and Cindy turned around, both swivelling gracefully on their heels. Like all of the Drake women aside from Zoe, they were delicate and feminine. Jade, her eldest sister, wore the stylish conservative clothes of the young soccer-mom-in-training; Cindy had on a sharp designer suit that fit her job as a PR executive.

'Zoe,' Jade said and leaned forward to give her a light, perfumed hug. Her younger sister hugged her, too, though more briskly, as befit a successful businesswoman.

'It's been ages,' said Jade, as sweetly as she always said everything. 'When are you going to come out to Fairfield and visit us? Kelsey and Justin would love to see their auntie.'

'I'll bring the cab by the next time I have a fare out there,' Zoe lied.

She knew when Nick came up next to her, partly because she felt a warming and excitement of the air, partly because of the breath of freshness that seemed to cling to his body, and partly because both her sisters' eyes widened.

Jade might be happily married with two toddlers and Cindy might have half the male population of New York at her feet, but neither one of them minded having a good look at a prime specimen of man. Zoe guessed that was one family trait she'd inherited, at least.

'Jade, Cindy, this is Nick,' Zoe said, and watched as her gorgeous sisters beamed all their blonde beauty in Nick's direction. Nick smiled, obviously dazzled, and held out his hand to them.

'Nick, these are my sisters,' Zoe said unhappily, watching him shake hands with each of them in turn. 'Is Di already here?'

Jade and Cindy were bound to know where their second eldest sister was; the three of them were practically attached by mobile phone.

'She's upstairs with Mom and Dad,' Cindy answered, not tearing her eyes away from Nick's handsome face.

The elevator dinged. 'Well, we might as well go up,' Zoe said. She restrained the urge to put her arm through Nick's in the sort of possessive gesture she often saw her mom and her two older sisters making with their men. There wasn't any point. He wasn't her possession, and he never would be, and Jade and Cindy would never believe her even if she pretended.

When they stepped in the elevator Zoe could see that her sisters were dying to ask all about Nick. They were holding it in well, though. Jade was arranging her pretty face into the sombre expression appropriate for a reading of one's great-aunt's will, and Cindy wasn't about to break etiquette if Jade didn't first.

'Poor Aunt Xenia,' she said instead, softly.

'I don't know,' said Zoe, irritated, because Cindy hadn't spent more than four hours with Xenia in the past five years, as far as Zoe knew. 'Getting killed while doing a skateboarding stunt was a pretty classy way to go. I bet she was pleased.'

'Zoe,' Jade said, more for form's sake than because she could ever possibly be shocked by anything that Zoe said.

'Really,' Zoe said. 'I bet she's up in heaven laughing her ass off. Nick and I were just talking about it, weren't we Nick?'

She heard the possessiveness in her voice, as blatant as the gesture she'd resisted, and winced.

'We were, and it does seem like a good way to go,' Nick said genially, and Zoe was immediately fifty times as irritated because Jade and Cindy didn't demur against Nick's comment and it seemed as if she needed him for backup. Which she didn't.

Zoe made a mental note not to ask Nick anything else. Her family would be all too glad to see her depending on a man.

The elevator dinged and they all went into the plushly carpeted hallway, and down it to the lawyers' office. Zoe hadn't been here before, but she guessed if you had to choose a lawyer it made sense to choose one who was rich, because they obviously had to be good at their stuff to earn all that money. Nick opened the glossy door for them as if he'd been opening doors for women all his life—he probably had; he had that whole 'shining armour and white charger thing' going on—and Jade and Cindy glided in as if men had been opening doors for them all their lives, which they had, of course. Zoe filed in after them, her hands on her hips.

Her mother and father and other sister Di were all in the waiting room, sitting on leather chairs. They stood when the four of them came in and there was the obligatory hugging session. Zoe suffered it.

'Oh, Jade, you look stunning,' her mother said, fingering Jade's cashmere cardigan, and then turning to Cindy with a smile. 'And that suit is beautiful, Cynthia. Zoe, it's so nice to see you in a skirt.'

Zoe caught the subtext. *We expected to see you in ratty old jeans, and that skirt isn't much better.*

'Bought it at a yard sale,' she said. 'Three bucks. Are we ready to go in and hear this will thing?'

'Who's your friend, Cindy?' Michael Drake asked his youngest daughter.

His smile was indulgent. Zoe had no doubt that her parents

spent many a pleasurable evening discussing their youngest daughter's bevy of beaus. They'd done the same thing about Jade and Di, while Zoe had been still living at home and her two older sisters had still been unmarried.

The only beau Zoe had ever brought home had been one of the guys who hung around near the railway tracks racing dirt bikes when she was about fifteen. Her parents had talked about him, all right.

Cindy was attractively confused at her father's mistake. 'Oh, Dad, I don't—'

'Mr Drake, Mrs Drake,' Nick said, stepping forward and extending his hand to Zoe's parents, 'I'm Nicholas Giroux. Zoe brought me here to see if there was anything relevant to my family in Ms Drake's will.'

'Zoe?' He concealed it well, but Zoe saw that, while her father had looked indulgent talking to Cindy, he looked wary talking to her. 'You think your aunt Xenia had something to do with this young man's family?'

'Let's face it, none of us had the slightest idea what she was up to,' Zoe said with as much cheerfulness as she could muster. 'There's some evidence she might have known Nick's dad. Nick's been staying with me in Xenia's apartment,' she added, and was rewarded by the surprised expressions on all of her family's faces.

At that moment the big wooden door on the side wall opened and a tubby man in a very expensive-looking suit came out. 'Mr and Mrs Drake, Jade, Diana, Zoe, Cynthia? Would you care to come in?'

Mr Feinberg shook each of their hands, including Nick's, as they came into his panelled office. He'd set up enough upholstered chairs for them all to be able to have a seat with a couple left over. The lawyer seemed nervous for some reason.

'I've copied the will for each of you,' he said, shifting from side to side on his tiny feet as he gave each of them a slim folder. 'It's not very complicated, it can be summed up quite quickly, and it will have to go through probate of course, especially with such a sizeable estate as Ms Drake's, but I feel her wishes are very clear.'

He took a seat behind his great glossy desk and cleared his throat. 'So, if you open your folders…'

Obediently, Zoe's family opened the cardboard folders. Zoe stared at the cover of hers. It was blue. Besides the funeral plan, it was the last message her great-aunt had left for her.

She wasn't in a hurry to read it.

Beside her, she heard Nick draw in a sharp breath. When she looked over she saw he'd opened his folder to the last page.

He held it out so she could see it, and pointed to the date on the bottom, underneath Xenia's bold black signature. 'April twenty-third,' he said.

'So?'

That wasn't long ago. It was unsettling to think that her great-aunt might have had a premonition of her own mortality just a few days before she'd bailed on her board.

'That's the same day my father's letter was postmarked.'

Zoe met Nick's dark eyes with her own.

'So,' said Mr Feinberg, clearing his throat, 'as I said, Ms Drake's wishes are clear. You can skip the legal language, and turn to page two, where Ms Drake bequeaths the sum of ten thousand dollars to her nephew Michael Drake, and stipulates that additional sums of ten thousand dollars to be invested in bonds for each of her four great-great nieces and nephews already born, with directions for an additional fifty thousand dollars to be set aside for children not yet born, to be held until their eighteenth birthdays when the monies may be used for college tuition or whatever other purpose the recipient desires.'

Jade and Di murmured to each other. Zoe, cynically, knew what they were talking about. Ten thousand dollars a kid wasn't bad, plus money for kids who hadn't been born, but to Xenia a hundred thousand dollars couldn't be more than a token amount. All of Xenia's living relatives were here in this room, and none of them except for Zoe's dad had received anything directly.

Zoe smiled. She just bet that Xenia had written her will in the way that would pique her relatives the most. Xenia had never shown any signs of wanting to please the rest of the Drake family, and Zoe was glad she was carrying it on in her will, too.

'If you turn to page three,' Mr Feinberg said, 'you'll see the main part of the will, where Ms Drake bequeaths all her remaining property, money, and concerns to her great-niece Zoe Drake.'

Zoe's head snapped up. She stared at the lawyer.

He cleared his throat again. 'It's quite a substantial estate, Ms Drake. You're named as the executor, as well, so we will need to go through the particulars together, and of course there's probate to consider, but with property and investments and income it's worth in the region of fifty million dollars.'

Zoe thought her family was probably talking, but she couldn't hear anything because as soon as the lawyer's words registered in her brain her ears filled with a rushing sound. Her entire body felt cold and hot at the same time. She stood and walked out of the office and through the waiting room.

The stairs were at the end of the corridor. She pushed open the fire door and into the concrete stairwell, taking the steps down two at a time. She watched her feet in her running shoes hitting each step precisely in the middle and concentrated on her knees flexing, her thigh muscles stretching and contracting. The metal railing was cold underneath her hand.

The office was on the twelfth floor. By the time Zoe got to the bottom of the staircase her legs were burning but her breath was still coming steady. She slammed the door open, strode across the lobby, and out into the street.

She wanted to sweat, to breathe hard, to feel right in her working body. She broke into a run as soon as she hit the sidewalk, doing her best to ignore how her skirt got in the way.

Two blocks down she felt a hand land on her shoulder. Zoe spun, her breathing finally sharp, her hands whipping up to defend herself.

It was Nick.

'Zoe, are you all right?'

She saw his dark eyes frowning and full of concern, his hair in disarray from running. She noticed she still clutched the blue folder containing Xenia's will in her right hand.

'Me?' she said. 'I'm just dandy. Didn't you hear the man? I'm a millionaire.'

She burst into tears.

CHAPTER FIVE

NICK PUT HIS arm around Zoe's shoulders and steered her across the busy street and into Central Park. Maybe she could carry on a conversation in the middle of a sidewalk, but he couldn't.

He was looking at the traffic and then looking for somewhere to sit down, but he could feel her body trembling under his arm. She didn't make a single sound, not a sniff or a whimper. Just these silent sobs shaking her body. Nick found a patch of grass under a tree, as isolated as they were going to get, and gently sat her down.

She looked straight ahead, not at him, still crying. He'd seen plenty of women crying in his life and Zoe wasn't like any of them. She didn't screw up her face or hitch in hysterical breaths. Her generous mouth was turned down at the corners in unhappiness, and fat tears gathered in her eyes, spilled over, and rolled down her cheeks, leaving wet trails on her skin. The tears made her eyes look bigger and bluer. They clumped her eyelashes together, darkening them.

He reached over and wiped the tears from her cheeks. Her skin was much softer than he'd expected.

'It was a surprise, huh?' he said.

'That's an understatement.' Her voice was even lower and huskier than usual. She swiped at her eyes, but the tears kept coming.

Nick's arm was still around her; he pulled her a little closer, as if he could protect her from her hurt with his body. She wasn't exactly pliant in his arms, but he could feel both the strength of her body and the soft pressure of her breast against his side.

'I'm sorry you lost your great-aunt,' he said.

'Why'd she leave her money to me?' She turned her head to look him in the face.

'Who else was she going to leave it to? You said she wasn't close to the rest of your family.'

'But why me? I barely knew her, too. She never even told me what she did for a living.' She wiped her eyes again, smearing moisture over her cheeks and clumping her eyelashes. It wasn't a delicate gesture, but it was a vulnerable one.

'It doesn't sound like she'd told anybody.'

'It's a lot of money, Nick. Really a lot. Why me?'

Nick tucked a strand of her hair back behind her ear. Her hair was silky and nearly as warm as her skin. 'Because she trusted you.'

'But *why?*' It came out as a wail, and Zoe bent her body to hide her face between her drawn-up knees. Her shoulders shook.

Nick stroked her back as she cried. She was wearing her horrible big leather jacket again but he could feel the shape of her back and shoulders through it. He remembered the sight of her next to her three sisters and her mother; all of the other female Drakes had been petite and narrow-shouldered. Zoe, with her straight posture and her determined stance, had seemed sturdy and more real. But under his hand now she felt fragile and feminine, maybe because she was crying.

He remembered how she'd stared at him this morning when he'd told her he trusted her not to lock him out of the house while he got breakfast. It was if he'd told her he had scientific evidence that the moon was made out of Alka-Seltzer. He was a relative stranger; he could understand why she'd be suspicious of his motives. It was harder to understand why she wouldn't accept that her great-aunt had faith in her.

Then again, he remembered how Zoe's mother had made the comment about her skirt, as if she were surprised that Zoe had made any effort with her clothing at all.

Maybe it wasn't so hard to figure out why Zoe didn't believe her relatives would trust her.

Her hair was tousled on the back of her head. He ran his fingers through it to straighten it, and again was surprised by how silky it was. In the sun shining through the leaves it was golden. He twisted a strand of it around his finger, interested in how it reflected the light and caressed his skin.

'Sometimes we just trust people,' he said to her, though he wasn't sure she was listening. 'Your great-aunt must have thought you were the person who deserved what she had. From the way you defended her personal things from me this morning, I'd say she was right.'

Zoe drew in a sharp breath and straightened, pulling away from him. She shook her head and rubbed her hands hard over her face.

'I don't believe I'm crying in front of you,' she said, her voice full of disgust.

'It's okay. I'm good with crying women. My sister used to spend a lot of time crying when we were growing up.'

Her face flushed and her eyes flashed, and Nick saw that she'd gone in a moment from sorrow to embarrassment to anger.

'Oh, well, aren't I lucky, to be in the presence of the expert in crying women.'

'I didn't mean that.'

'What did you mean, then? You're glad to have the opportunity to show what a nice guy you are by comforting the poor little heiress when she's upset about her auntie leaving her fifty million dollars? What are you going to do next, offer to buy me an ice cream with a cherry on top?'

'Zoe, be reasonable. You're upset. I was talking to you. That's all.'

She jumped to her feet. 'So now you're a nice, *reasonable* guy. Gee, your life must be good, especially with all those crying women to put your arm around.' She brushed the grass of her skirt with savage movements. 'Well, Mr Boy Scout, I don't need your comfort or your trees or your reasonableness. I'm just fine on my own.'

And with that she turned on the heel of her running shoe and sprinted off.

* * *

This time, waiting in the hallway, Nick wasn't as patient.

He sat back against the wall, his arms crossed on his chest, his foot tapping on the carpeted floor. Zoe had been gone for over three hours now and his backpack, which contained his wallet, was behind that locked door.

When she'd run off he'd let her, figuring she'd burn off a little steam and then come back. After half an hour under the tree he'd decided to look in the direction she'd run in, but although he was reasonably competent at tracking people and animals in the wilderness it was totally impossible in New York if he didn't know where she was headed. He'd jogged a couple blocks, seen a subway station, realised she could be anywhere in the city by now, and slowly walked back to Xenia's apartment.

Where he'd been sitting waiting for her ever since, his blood getting hotter and hotter.

She was impossible, aggressive, capricious, and sarcastic, and she had no right to lash out at him for doing nothing but trying to make her feel better.

She had no reason to run off and leave him.

Nick got up and paced the length of the hallway. He was hungry and thirsty and fed up and if she didn't show up with the keys to the apartment soon he was going to break the door down. Then she'd see what a 'nice guy' he was.

He swore and punched the tastefully papered wall. Why was this woman winding him up so much? He'd only known her a couple of days, and only by chance. He'd tried to help her and she'd thrown it back in his face, and that should be the end of it.

If the keys to his truck didn't happen to be locked behind that door, he'd be out of New York, father or no father.

The elevator dinged and Nick whirled around. Zoe stepped out, and he strode towards her.

'Listen,' he started, and then he stopped both talking and walking, because Zoe had changed.

She wore low-slung faded jeans that fit her as if they'd been made for her, and a bright pink T-shirt that clung to her top. The shapeless black jacket had been replaced by a tight brown leather jacket that followed the curve of her waist.

These were her own clothes, clothes that fit her body. And she had a good body.

No, not just good. A great body.

She was slim-hipped and strong-shouldered, but she had just enough curves to make her incredibly feminine. Her waist was slender, her legs long and obviously muscular underneath the faded blue jeans. The firm lines of her limbs contrasted with the soft roundness of her breasts and the lushness of her mouth.

Nick swallowed, all the angry words he'd been meaning to say deserting him.

'Hi,' he said. 'You look good.'

Which was an understatement, as well as a revelation.

She was carrying a big canvas bag over one shoulder and a carrier bag in one hand; she put them down and scratched the back of her neck as if she were uncomfortable.

'So it's like this,' she said. 'I hate people seeing me crying. So I got mad.'

He remembered the look of utter humiliation that had crossed her face when she'd looked up from her knees, tears streaking her face. Until this moment, he'd been too angry to think about what it might mean.

'Okay,' he said.

'I also hate being condescended to.'

Condescending to her? The most ornery woman in New York?

Wisely, Nick remembered that Zoe was attempting some sort of apology and he restrained his answer. 'I wasn't trying to be condescending.'

'All right. I'll accept your apology.'

Nick couldn't help smiling at that. 'I don't think I've apologised.'

'Yeah, well, you're looking sorry.' She smiled at him and held out her hand. 'Truce?'

'Truce.'

He'd shaken her hand before, and hadn't noticed how her grip was firm and her skin was warm and smooth. He did this time.

'So, you're waiting out here for your dad still.' Her expression was back to teasing. 'I take it he hasn't shown up yet, or I wouldn't have to worry about seeing you again.'

'He hasn't shown up yet. I was waiting for you. All my stuff, including my money, is in the apartment.'

She nodded. 'Bet you're hungry.'

'Bet I am.'

'You should remember that before you piss me off next time,' she said, but she winked. 'I've got some groceries so we can make something to eat.'

'Good.' He didn't move. 'Did you come back for any reason besides getting an apology from me?'

She shrugged. 'I thought about it on the way back to my apartment in the Bronx. I've got to take some time off work to sort out Xenia's funeral and I figure I'll help you find your dad while I'm at it. And it's going to be easier to look through Xenia's papers properly if I'm staying here.' She pulled the apartment keys out of her jacket pocket.

'You said this morning it was too private.'

'That was before I knew Xenia left everything to me. I figure if she didn't want me to see something, she'd have gotten rid of it.'

'Thanks,' he said, and he was rewarded by the sight of her smile, white teeth against pink lips.

'No problem. One of us might as well get something worthwhile out of this whole inheritance thing.'

'Besides the fifty million dollars?'

'Xenia knew I didn't want her money,' she said quietly. 'I don't want it now.'

'Maybe that's why she left it to you.'

'I wish she hadn't.' She compressed her mouth, and shook her head as if she was clearing it. 'Anyway, this talking isn't going to get you fed.'

'It certainly isn't.' He bent and picked up her canvas bag,

and grunted at its unexpected weight. 'What have you got in here, bricks?'

'Dumb-bells. I use them for training.' She took hold of the strap and tugged it away from him. 'I can handle it.'

He considered arguing about it, but their truce was too new and, besides, he liked the way the straining of her arm and back muscles made her breasts thrust forward. He gave it to her, and she slung it onto her shoulder and picked up the carrier bag.

'By the way, I'm curious,' she said, unlocking the door. 'Did you see how my family reacted to the news that I've inherited fifty million dollars? I wasn't looking.'

'They were pretty surprised.'

That was an understatement. Every one of the Drakes had been in eye-bugging, jaw-dropping shock. The youngest sister Cindy had actually gasped when the lawyer had made the announcement.

Zoe let out a sharp laugh as she went into the apartment, Nick close behind her. 'Yeah, I bet they were surprised.' They reached the kitchen and Zoe dropped the bags and turned to him, a smile on her lips. It was wide, lopsided, and naughty.

'I bet they think I'm going to go right out and blow the whole inheritance in Vegas or something. Come to think of it, that would really piss them off.' She bit her lip and looked as if she were considering it.

Nick laughed. 'It would take serious dedication to lose fifty million dollars in Vegas.'

'That's true. Maybe I should do something requiring much less effort.' She began pulling packages from the grocery bag. 'Did you see how they looked at me when they thought I was shacking up with you in my dear departed great-aunt's apartment?'

'I did. Why didn't you tell them the whole truth?'

She shrugged. 'I guess I can never disappoint them if I confirm their worst suspicions, right?' She held up a package of pasta. 'Spaghetti all right with you?'

'Somehow I didn't expect my first meal with a multimillion-airess to be spaghetti.'

'Hey, you can take the girl out of the Bronx but you can't take the Bronx out of the girl.' She pulled out a head of lettuce and a tomato and tossed them in a high arc in his direction. 'In honour of your apology, I'll even let you make the salad.'

Nick caught the lettuce in one hand and the tomato in the other. Zoe bent to get some pots and pans out of a cupboard, affording him a view of her shapely behind. Nick couldn't help but stare.

She most definitely wasn't his type. Nick liked delicate, small women. Women he could tuck under his arm, carry things for, feel tall and protective next to. Women with small hands and feet and high voices and soft bodies. Women, as a matter of fact, a lot like Zoe's sisters.

But Zoe had something, all right. Enough of something for him to want to cross the kitchen and put his hands all over her.

More than that, actually. He wanted to cross the kitchen, turn her around to face him, bury one hand in her golden hair, spread the other against her perfect backside, and kiss her senseless. And then he wanted to lift her onto the kitchen counter and pull those jeans down her long, strong legs.

'We can look through Xenia's desk after supper,' she said.

Her voice brought him back to reality. Fortunately, she was turned away from him so she couldn't see what his little spontaneous fantasy had done to him. Quickly, he pulled out a chair and sat himself and his raging erection down at the kitchen table.

'So what are you going to do when you see your dad again?' she asked, and he welcomed the opportunity to think about something other than her wrapping those legs around his waist.

'I want to ask him why he left and didn't come back. And I want to tell him what he did to us. You know, my sister was convinced for a long time that he left us because she wasn't good enough.'

Nick shook his head, remembering how fierce he'd felt when Kitty had told him that, one tearful night after her high-school prom. 'She spent a long time feeling that she could never succeed; she went through a divorce and everything.'

'Does she want to see your dad, too?'

'I called her to tell her I was coming down here and she was okay with it, but she says she's past it now. She's gotten married again and she's really happy. I think she feels that love conquers everything, even a bad parent.'

She opened a can of tomatoes with quick, agile turns of her wrist. 'Do you agree?'

'I think that love would have to be pretty damn special to conquer everything.'

'You're right. It would.' She held a knife out to him by the handle. 'You going to do any work, Boy Scout? I thought you were hungry.'

Fortunately, talking about his father had deflated his arousal pretty effectively. Nick stood, took the knife, and brought his vegetables to the counter where she'd set up a chopping board for him. He was standing close to her, and for the first time he noticed she had a clean, citrusy scent. She must have put on perfume at her apartment, as well as changed her clothes.

He imagined stepping closer to her and pressing his lips against the column of her throat and breathing in more of that perfume.

Uh, uh. Down, Nick.

Talking about his father had distracted him from desire, but it should tell him something else, too. He was only in New York for a short time. And he had no intention of striking up a relationship with somebody whom he'd be leaving soon. He wasn't that kind of a guy.

He'd spent nearly twenty-four hours in Zoe's presence without noticing that he was attracted to her. He'd just have to un-notice it.

CHAPTER SIX

PLEASE, LORD, MAKE him have some clothes on.

Zoe sent up the quick prayer as she walked into the building, waved at Ralph, and waited for the elevator to come.

She'd been doing so well for the past twenty-four hours. She'd managed the afternoon and the evening with Nick constantly by her side without jumping on him. Of course, her hands had been full most of the time because she'd been going through the papers in her great-aunt's desk and study, but having her hands full had never stopped her from making a fool of herself in the past.

And her great-aunt's papers weren't exactly a distraction. For somebody who had seemed to lead as interesting a life as Xenia's, her personal effects were distinctly ordinary. No juicy letters, no diaries, not even a computer. Zoe hadn't found much more than bills, and while Nick had pointed out that the phone bills might, eventually, direct them towards Eric Giroux, Zoe had also pointed out that they would have to call every number listed on them to find out. Nothing else seemed even remotely connected to Nick's father.

And just as importantly, nothing gave her any clues about why her great-aunt had given her everything.

On the personal restraint side, though, she'd done okay. She hadn't touched, she hadn't drooled, she'd barely stared, even through dinner, when she'd had to sit across from him and endure the horrific torture of being reminded that this man was very sexy when he ate.

She had, even, beyond all expectations, managed to sleep knowing that his body was in the boxroom next to hers, separated from her by a single internal wall.

And then this morning, of course, he'd taken a damn shower.

The elevator doors dinged and Zoe went inside, crossing her arms over her breasts in some pathetic form of self-control, because the memory of seeing Nick wet from the shower on his way from the bathroom to his room, water clinging to the dark hair on his head and on his chest, smelling of warmth and soap and shaving foam, made her want to both melt and scream.

Which was, of course, why she'd gone running out of the apartment and spent the entire day sorting out errands for tomorrow's funeral. Errands that the funeral-home guys could have done just as easily. She was so desperate to stay away from Nick that she'd even forced herself to spend a couple of hours shopping for a black outfit that fitted her.

No, you didn't do that to stay away from him, a voice in her mind said. *You did it so that you would look decent at the funeral tomorrow in front of him.*

'Shut up,' she said aloud to herself. She'd bought the clothes to show respect for her great-aunt Xenia at the funeral. Not to please Nick, not to please her family, not even to please herself.

The elevator opened and Zoe tossed her head to dispel these thoughts and went down the hallway to the apartment. She had to admit, it was a hell of a lot nicer than the hallway in her building in the Bronx. There wasn't even a hint of a mouse. But it didn't feel right to her. It didn't feel hers.

'Hey, I'm home!' she yelled as soon as she opened the door. Nick could be out—they'd arranged for Ralph to let him in and out of the apartment—but if he was in, she wanted to make damn sure that he was dressed.

Then again, her being around didn't seem to stop him from disrobing, and why would it? He obviously didn't register her as a person of the opposite sex.

'In here,' she heard him call from the living room. When she got there he was sitting on the couch, reading a paperback. She dropped her bags, collapsed into an armchair, and stretched out her feet, which ached even in her running shoes.

'Find your father yet?' she asked.

'No. I asked around and nobody's seen or heard of him. If he doesn't show up to your great-aunt's funeral tomorrow it looks like I don't have any more leads.'

Zoe nodded. If he was out of leads, that meant he'd be leaving. Which was good.

So how come her throat was immediately burning with disappointment?

'Everything is sorted out for the funeral,' she said. 'Except for one thing that's annoying. I got the wrong shoes.' She pulled a photocopy from the pocket of her jeans. 'Apparently the black Vuitton heels were meant to be in a box.'

Nick had lowered the paperback and was looking at her. She'd noticed him looking at her like that a few times last night, too: searching her face, then letting his eyes survey her body. If she were the type to have crazy unrealistic hopes she would almost think that he was checking her out.

But as she wasn't that type, she thought he was probably trying to figure out why she didn't look more like her sisters.

'Xenia should have asked one of my sisters to find her clothes,' she said, something twisting in her gut. 'They were born knowing about fashion.'

'I think your great-aunt probably had other qualities in mind when she chose you.'

Anger rose in Zoe, stronger even than lust. *Other qualities.* Was that supposed to be some sort of consolation prize? For not being sexy, not being smart, not being successful?

Zoe jumped to her feet. She'd decided not to be mad at him any more, but he really could push it.

'Nick, I told you not to be condescending,' she said, her voice loud in her ears. 'You don't know a damn about why my great-aunt chose me. If you're so hot on trying to figure out family motivations, why don't you concentrate on why your father chose to leave you?'

She started to walk out of the room, leaving her bags behind, but as she passed a side table she heard a noise that made her stop.

There was a big cardboard box on the table that hadn't been there before. And there was something moving around inside it, something scratching and making low, throaty noises.

'What the hell is this?' she said.

Nick didn't answer. She looked at him and saw that he hadn't straightened his slouch on the sofa, but he was tense and gazing into her eyes.

'I know why my father left me,' he said. 'Because he was a coward who preferred to let his ten-year-old son take care of his family. You, on the other hand, are an adult and I imagine your great-aunt had good reasons to trust you. You can get as angry about it as you want, but it's not my fault she left you the money and you feel guilty about it.'

For a moment she just stared at him. She had a feeling as if her will had met something just as strong in the middle of the room, and they were at a deadlock.

'Just don't talk down to me,' she said.

'I wasn't talking down to you. I wouldn't dare to, especially with the way you take pot-shots at me when you're angry. I was saying what I thought. And you brought it up in the first place.'

Beside her, whatever was in the box scratched and gurgled again. There was something dark in Nick's eyes. She was glad to take her gaze away from his and look at the box.

'What have you brought in here?'

'Open it up and see. Be careful, though.'

Gingerly she peeled back the lid of the box and looked inside. She saw two beady eyes, a beak, and a greeny-grey feathered throat.

'It's a pigeon,' she said in surprise and disgust.

'Yes.'

She looked more closely and saw that both its feet were wrapped in little white bandages.

'Nick. You're playing doctor to a pigeon?'

'It had abscesses on both its feet, which I treated.' Nick joined her at the box. 'I had a hell of a time catching it. I've had an easier time catching cormorants. New York must make the animals suspicious.'

'Nick, why are you rescuing a pigeon? They're pests: there are trillions of them.'

'You don't think I should help a pigeon because it's a pest?'

'Yes! This isn't some endangered species on some island somewhere.'

'All right.' He picked up a pair of gloves lying next to the box. 'I'll kill it.' He reached into the box.

'Don't!'

Nick paused. 'If it's a pest, why can't I kill it?'

'Because—' Zoe tried to think of a reason, and couldn't. 'Just don't.'

'Look,' Nick said, his voice calm, his hands still in the box with the pigeon, 'I won't let an animal suffer, no matter what kind of animal it is. I can cure it, or I can kill it. Which one do you want me to do?'

Once again, it was his will, iron-strong, against hers, except this time he had a life in his hands.

'Why are you so damn responsible?' she growled.

'Why do you deny that you can be?' he shot back.

Silently, not moving or touching, they wrestled with each other.

In the end, giving in was easier than answering his question. If Nick's only options were curing something or killing it, he wouldn't understand her answer, anyway.

He wouldn't understand how if there was something wrong with you, you learned to live with it, to shrug it off.

'Just don't let it crap on the furniture,' she said, and turned away. She'd nearly got to the door when she heard him say, 'Thanks.'

The box was huge. No wonder she'd missed it the first time she'd gone in the closet; she'd been looking for shoes, and this box was big enough to hold a television. But it said Louis Vuitton, printed on it in big black letters, and it was the only box that did.

It was right in the back of the closet, and too big to open in there surrounded by clothes, so Zoe cleared shoes out of the way and dragged it out into the centre of the bedroom. She sat on the carpet next to it, looking it over. Whatever shoes were in that box were either made for a giant, or made out of lead.

'Sounds like you're heaving the furniture around in here.'

Nick was in the doorway and it had only been ten minutes since she'd seen him and argued with him and her heart thumped as if she'd been missing him for years. How come she wanted him so much, pigeon-rescuer, nature-lover, good-deed-doing Boy Scout?

'Apparently this is the shoe box.' She picked at the packing tape, but her nails weren't long enough to get a grip.

'Here.' Nick stepped forward and pulled a Swiss Army knife from his pocket. He offered to cut the tape for her, but Zoe held her hand out for the knife so he gave it to her instead.

'Very impressed you pack a knife,' she said, making short work of the tape.

'I was using it to cut bandages. This box doesn't only have shoes in it, does it?'

'Doubtful.' She pulled the top open.

On top there was a pair of shoes and a cream envelope, one of Xenia's personalised ones, with the name 'Zoe' written on it in Xenia's black script. Zoe took out the shoes and the envelope and laid them to one side while she looked in the box.

It was a stack of hardcover books. Two by two, Zoe removed them and put them on the carpet. There were dozens of them. They all had similar jacket designs, a stylised photograph on a black background and the author's name in blood-red capital letters.

Zoe had seen the books before, in shops, libraries, being read on the subway, but never before in this apartment.

'Well I'll be,' she said, shaking her head, looking at the collection of books.

Nick sat down next to her. He seemed to be a little breathless.

'Your great-aunt was Xander Dark,' he said.

Zoe looked from the books to the envelope on the carpet.

'Xander Dark' was huge in blood-red letters on the books. 'Xenia Drake' was in discreet engraving on the envelope.

Zoe threw her head back and laughed. Great belly laughs, holding on to her stomach, tears squeezing out of her eyes.

'My great-aunt,' she gasped, 'was one of the most famous horror writers in America.'

Nick picked up the copy of *If You Go Down To The Woods…*

'I know now why she had the bear trap,' he said, looking from the photograph of a bear trap on the jacket to the real thing in the glass case beside them.

'And the chain-saw.' Zoe giggled, pointing at the cover of *Chain Reaction.*

Nick turned to the back inside flap of the book jacket. '"Xander Dark is the best-selling author of over thirty chilling novels of suspense and horror,"' he read. 'No photograph, no biographical information, nothing. Did she really keep this a secret from everyone?'

'It's certainly a secret from me and the rest of the family.' Zoe shook her head in admiration. 'What a woman.'

'She went to a lot of effort to hide it. There aren't even any horror novels on her bookshelves.'

'She wanted me to find out, though.' Zoe picked up the envelope and carefully tore it open, removing the single heavy sheet of paper.

Darling Zoe,

I'll bet you never suspected that your old great-aunt was the 'Master of Murder, Mayhem, and Monsters'.

I need you to do two things for me, sweetheart, and then you can do as you like, as you always so wonderfully do. I'd like you to give my bear trap to my agent, Gabriella Hernandez, and my thumbscrew collection to my editor, Hector Banner. Both of them will appreciate the aptness. Gabriella, Hector and Saul Feinberg are, by the way, the only other three people who know the true identity of Xander Dark.

My secret, and the rest of my belongings, are yours to

do with as you will. Enjoy, my precious girl. We're two of
a kind, you and I.
    With my love,
    Xenia

For the second time in two days, Zoe felt tears rushing into
her eyes.

We're two of a kind, you and I.

They weren't. Her great-aunt had been glamorous, successful, talented, beautiful, intelligent. And yet the fact that her great-
aunt had thought they were similar, at least for as long as it had
taken her to write that sentence, was precious.

A tear fell onto the letter. Zoe looked up sharply and began
to jump to her feet. She wasn't going to cry in front of Nick again.

But Nick had left and closed the door after him.

'Well, well, well. A man who can iron, eh?'

Nick glanced up from the ironing board he'd set up in the
kitchen. Carefully, he set the iron down. The thing was hot and
if he held it while looking at Zoe, he was bound to get burned.

'Wow,' he said, feeling slightly singed anyway. 'You look great.'

She wore a black skirt, but it wasn't her yard sale one; this
one was slim and ended just above her knees and showed off her
long, toned legs, especially since she was wearing heels. He
dragged his gaze up from her bare legs, though the rest of her
wasn't any less tempting because she wore a clingy black top and
a form-fitting black velvet jacket.

'You went shopping?' he asked, noticing his voice wasn't all
that steady.

She shrugged. 'I figured if Xenia was going to be wearing
Gaultier, I should make an effort.'

'Good effort.' He pulled off his T-shirt and reached for the
shirt he'd just finished ironing.

Zoe burst into a gale of coughing. He stepped forward, his
hand outstretched to thump her on the back. 'Are you all right?'

'Fine,' she spluttered, and clapped her hand over her mouth.

'Just—a tickly throat.' She turned her back on him and leaned on her hands on the counter, clearing her throat.

'This is the second shirt I've ironed today.' He unplugged the iron and pulled on his warm shirt. Not as warm as her skin would be.

'Let me guess,' she said, taking down a bowl and pouring cereal in it, her back turned to him. 'You got bird poop all over the other one.'

'The pigeon is certainly generous, though I'd rather tangle with that bird than a wounded skunk.' He began to do up the buttons. 'The pigeon is better this morning, by the way.'

'Oh, I am relieved. I didn't feel like having more than one funeral today.'

She seemed to be taking her time pouring milk and coffee, and Nick wondered if something was wrong. He'd tried to stay out of her way all last evening, partly because he'd thought she'd need the space after reading whatever her great-aunt had to say, partly because she'd looked so incredibly sexy, lying there laughing on the bedroom floor, her eyes bright and her mouth wide, that he'd thought he should remove himself from temptation.

Of course, she could be upset about her great-aunt's funeral.

The ironing board made a screeching sound as he folded it up, and Zoe turned around. She had an enormous smile on her face.

'I am so looking forward to this funeral,' she said.

So much for that idea.

'Why?'

She brought her breakfast to the table and sat down. 'You and I, Nicholas Giroux, are two of only five living people who know that Xenia was Xander Drake. Everybody at that funeral is going to be looking around and wondering where Xenia got all her money. Including my family.' She took a huge spoonful of cereal, smiling as she chewed.

Nick sat across from her. 'You're not going to tell them, are you?'

'Nope.' She chuckled as she demolished her breakfast. Nick couldn't help but enjoy watching her eat; her no-nonsense hunger was somehow incredibly sensual.

She was nearly finished when she looked up suddenly. 'I just thought of something. The letter my great-aunt wrote me was dated the same as her will. April twenty-third.'

'The same date my father's letter was mailed. What do you think the connection could be? Do you think they were together that day? Do you think my father had something to do with her will? It's a very recent will, after all.'

'Maybe. Then again, if I were taking up skateboarding at age seventy-four I'd write my will, too.' Her blue eyes met his. 'It does seem to point to the probability that he'll be at her funeral, though. Are you ready to meet him?'

'I've been ready to meet him for sixteen years.' Nick heard his voice had turned grim. Zoe's eyes narrowed slightly as she looked at him, as if she were trying to figure something out.

She scraped back her chair. 'Well, it looks like it'll be a happy family day all round. Are you ready? I want to get there a couple minutes early to make sure everything's the way Xenia wanted it.'

And he'd accused her of avoiding responsibility; clearly not with this. He found himself proud of her. 'Just need to put on a tie.'

'And I just need to brush my teeth. Meet you at the front door in five.'

When she met him she smelled of toothpaste, but she'd also put on a bit of lip gloss that made her mouth look even more delicious.

He offered his arm. 'Shall we go, Ms Drake?'

For a split second he thought she was going to take it, and that would be a pleasure, too, but then she raised a cynical eyebrow. 'I can walk in heels, you know. I'm not that hopeless at being a woman.'

'No, you're very good at being a woman.'

She didn't answer him, just concentrated on opening the door and locking it after them, and he wondered if she'd heard what he said, or understood what he'd meant. He'd never met a woman more reluctant to hear compliments than Zoe Drake.

Or maybe he wasn't so good at giving them. Maybe he needed to try a little harder.

At the desk, Ralph was wearing a suit instead of his normal uniform, and he nodded sombrely to Zoe's cheery, 'See you later!'

'He's devastated at losing her,' Zoe told Nick quietly as they went outside. 'Says she was his favourite. He couldn't find anybody to cover for him today but he's going to come to the funeral for half an hour on his lunch break.'

Nick remembered Ralph's sudden look of sadness, when he'd first said he was looking for Ms Drake, and despite the fact that the concierge still looked at him as if he were an unwanted piece of gum on his shoe Nick felt a little bit of sympathy for him.

'How are we getting to—?' he started, but Zoe had already raised her arm and let out a piercing whistle. A yellow cab swerved up to them and stopped, engine rattling. The side window rolled down and a loud, unmistakable wolf-whistle came out.

Nick frowned and leaned towards the driver, who was staring at Zoe with lascivious eyes. 'Hey, buddy, there's no need for—'

Zoe gently but firmly pushed Nick out of the way and stuck her head in the open window. 'Hey, José, how's it hanging, man?'

'Zoe, dude, you are looking H-O-T hot!' The driver licked his finger and pressed it to an imaginary surface, making a hissing sound.

Zoe laughed and opened the back door to get into the cab. Nick followed, knowing he shouldn't be bothered by Zoe's friend ogling her but being bothered anyway. He'd forgotten that Zoe drove a cab for a living, and forgetting this fact annoyed him, too.

'You going to your great-aunt's funeral, right?' José said, pulling the cab into traffic. 'I gotta radio the boys and tell them my man Zoe is wearing a skirt.'

'I'll never live this down,' Zoe said to Nick, sitting back with a huge grin.

'Are you going to keep driving a cab?' he asked her, quietly in case she hadn't told her colleagues yet.

'Of course.'

'Even though you're worth fifty million dollars? Do you like the job that much?'

'I'm not in love with it, but it's my job. I don't want to depend on my great-aunt for the rest of my life.'

That was an interesting way of thinking of it. 'Surely she

willed her estate to you because she wanted you to have it. That doesn't mean you're dependent on her.'

'And what else would you call it if I stopped working and lived off money that she earned?'

Nick paused, remembering a conversation he'd had with his mother years ago. Sue Giroux worked in a vet's office as a receptionist, a job she loved but that didn't pay much. When money was especially tight when they were kids, around Christmas or when a big bill came in, and before Nick and Kitty were old enough to be able to help out by getting part-time jobs, Sue used to work extra night and weekend shifts in a warehouse, packing magazines.

She never complained; Nick had never heard his mother complain in his life. But he remembered her getting home from the vet's office only to grab a quick dinner and then go out again to work until midnight. After a few days her face would look weary. After a few weeks she'd be walking like an old woman, her skin pale, even her hair duller. The only part of her that hadn't changed was the spark and fighting spirit in her eyes.

'Why don't you find him?' he asked her, when he was about fourteen years old. A couple of his friends at school had divorced parents; he'd heard about child support. 'He has to give you money, it's the law, right?'

His mother put down her cup of tea and stroked his hair back with a hand that was tired yet strong.

'Nicky, honey, you're right, it is the law. But we stopped depending on Daddy the minute he walked away from us, and he stopped depending on us, too. Being a father isn't about money, and nothing he could ever put in a bank account would bring him back.'

'But it's unfair,' he said, and, though his mother tried to argue and tease him out of it, he felt the unfairness too much to put it aside.

He still felt it now, though he understood his mother's pride, and he could understand Zoe's, too.

'What are you going to do with all of the money, then?' he asked. 'Keep it in a bank account somewhere? Will you live in your great-aunt's apartment?'

'No,' she said quickly. 'That's hers. And I don't know what I'm going to do with the money. I haven't thought about it yet.'

'Here we are, *chica*,' José said, pulling up in front of the biggest church Nick had ever seen. Although some of it was covered in scaffolding, he could still see that the front was crowded with carved statues and Gothic filigreed arches. He didn't get a chance to look at it closely because he saw José's eyes watching Zoe's bare legs in the rear-view mirror as she slid out of the cab.

'Thanks,' he said to José, knowing his voice held more than a little possessiveness as he held out a ten-dollar bill for the driver to take.

'Oh, no, it's only a few blocks, I wouldn't charge Zoe,' José said, holding up his hand to ward off the money.

Zoe leaned in the window again. 'Don't be stupid, José; you've got to earn a living like we all do. Here. Take it or I'll have to kick your ass.' She held out her own ten-dollar bill.

'It would be a pleasure to have my ass kicked by you,' said José, but he took Zoe's money, ignoring Nick's.

'I was paying for the cab,' he said to her when he got out, frowning.

'Hey, as you say, I'm a multimillionaire,' she said breezily, and climbed the steps with him to the church's grand entrance.

She certainly did know how to walk in high heels. With every step her hips had an extra sway that was one of the most seductive things he'd ever seen, all the more so for being unconscious. He wanted to put his hands on her hips and feel her movement, as well as see it.

Instead he stuffed his hands into the pockets of his trousers. It was a church. A funeral. No time for lustful thoughts.

CHAPTER SEVEN

THE CHURCH WAS huge. Inside its vast echoing space, Nick felt as small as a child.

'I can see why Xenia wanted to have her funeral here,' Zoe said, gazing at the enormous stained-glass windows, the elaborately carved stone, the soaring ceiling and the immense gleaming organ. Scaffolding spider-webbed up the inside walls, too. 'It's straight out of *The Addams Family*.'

'And that would make me Lurch,' said a voice from their left. Nick felt rather than saw Zoe start beside him as a man came out of the shadows.

He wasn't really kidding about the Lurch reference, Nick thought; he was very tall, very thin, and sunken-cheeked, dressed in the black of a clergyman. But his eyes were glittering with humour.

'Well, if you're Lurch, I'm Pugsley and this is Uncle Fester,' said Zoe cheerfully, going up to him with her hand outstretched.

Uncle Fester? Nick ran his hand over his head to make sure he wasn't suddenly bald as Zoe and the man of God got acquainted. From their conversation he could tell they had met before at one of Xenia's birthday parties, which were apparently famous all over Manhattan for their eclectic mix of people and the quality of the champagne. His name wasn't Lurch, it was John, and as he guided them through the church into a gilded side chapel set up for the funeral, Nick began to search his surroundings for a maybe-familiar figure.

He and Zoe had agreed: if Nick's father was in New York, he could be at this funeral. Xenia had expected well over a hundred guests.

Nick had been bang-awake since four this morning, an urgent feeling he couldn't quite name making his heart beat fast and his stomach feel queasy, his mind spinning on the idea that he might be seeing his father again. Zoe had distracted him before, but now the feeling intensified.

He peered around him. There were plenty of people in the church, strolling around, kneeling in prayer, sitting in the pews, and about a third of them were male. He stared at every man who was close to his father's age, questioning and weighing probabilities.

What colour would his hair be—grey or still dark? Would he even have any hair? Would he have gained weight, lost it, be healthy or sickly?

Nick remembered his father as tall and broad, a very big man—but then again Nick had been ten years old, and now he was over six feet himself. His mother and Kitty told him he resembled his father. Would it be like looking in a mirror, or stepping into a time machine?

He couldn't remember Eric Giroux's voice at all, although Nick remembered hearing it, could even remember some of the words his father had said. But the pitch of it, the timbre and the accent, was gone from his mind. He didn't think it had lasted much beyond his twelfth birthday.

Mostly, he remembered his father's hands. They were always rough and reddened from working outside. They were good at tying knots, chopping wood, creating flies for fishing, fixing things.

He looked down at his own hands, rough from working outside, good at catching animals, treating them, building shelters and paths, planting trees. Would this be how he knew his father, not from his face or his voice but from his hands?

Or maybe there would be an instant connection, not a recognition of features but something more basic. As if he saw an aspect of himself standing in front of him.

Nick frowned. None of the men he could see in the church

was the least bit familiar, either to his mind or to his feelings. But hardly any guests had arrived for the funeral yet. He shifted his attention back to Zoe.

She had shaken hands with John again and had turned into the side chapel. At the front was Xenia's gleaming mahogany coffin, surrounded by fountains of lilies and white roses. Nearby, Zoe's parents and three sisters stood with assorted men and children who he assumed were the sisters' partners and the young beneficiaries of Xenia's will.

It was almost imperceptible, but Nick saw Zoe straighten her spine and set her shoulders before she walked down the aisle to join them. Deciding he'd look for his father again in a few minutes, he followed her without waiting for an invitation.

'Zoe,' Mrs Drake said, stepping forward and giving her daughter a light hug and kiss on the cheek, 'are you all right? You ran out so quickly at the lawyer's.'

'I'm fine.'

'You've done a wonderful job arranging the funeral. And you look lovely.'

'Thanks.' Zoe's voice was cold.

From where he stood, Nick could see the expressions on both mother and daughter's faces: Zoe's smile had become strained, an imitation of her usual self-confident grin, and Mrs Drake's face showed pain at her daughter's rebuff before schooling itself back into a smile.

'Did you go shopping?' she asked.

This time, Nick could see the pain on Zoe's face, too—only for a split second—and he could tell she was catching a sub-text in her mother's words.

'Don't worry, I didn't blow the fifty million dollars yet.'

When Zoe turned away neither one of them looked happy. Their disappointed expressions, unguarded for a moment, were exactly the same.

He remembered what she'd said the two days before, after the reading of the will: *I guess I can never disappoint them if I confirm their worst suspicions, right?*

It looked as if he wasn't the only one who had some issues with a parent.

And he could see that Zoe's defensiveness, her inability to accept a compliment, didn't just apply to her relationship with him. It seemed as if her defences were something she'd learned a long time ago.

'Nicholas, was it?' Mr Drake had noticed him, and was regarding him with a wary eye. Nick nodded and put out his hand to shake.

'I'm sorry I had to leave without saying goodbye the other day, sir,' Nick said, 'or thanking you for allowing me to listen to the reading of Ms Drake's will.'

He nodded, and Nick had the impression his apology had fallen distinctly flat. 'I can't blame you for chasing after Zoe, of course. Especially after the news of her inheritance.'

Nick was catching some sub-text of his own. He chose to ignore it. 'It was a very emotional moment for her—' he began, but Zoe interrupted him.

'You're right, Dad, I'm bound to have all the men chasing after me now,' Zoe said loudly and cheerfully. 'Gosh, I must be the most eligible bachelorette in New York now that Aunt Xenia has died.'

'I wasn't expecting you to run out,' the eldest sister, Jade, said. 'I mean, it couldn't have been a surprise to you that she left you all your money. You were staying in her apartment already, weren't you?'

Zoe's smile got broader. 'Oh, Aunt Xenia's still full of surprises, believe me.'

'Do you have any idea of why she left everything to you?' the youngest sister asked. From the eager way she asked and the expressions in the rest of the family's eyes, Nick could tell it was a question that the Drakes had been discussing quite a bit over the past two days.

'I don't know,' Zoe said. Unlike her other answers, it was said without any defensiveness, and of course Nick knew that Zoe had been wondering as much as the rest of her family.

'I mean, it was such a shock,' Cindy continued. 'I just thought she would've left it to somebody more—'

'Cindy,' rebuked Jade.

The guardedness returned to Zoe's face.

'Responsible? Worthy? Someone who deserved it?' she said.

'Not that,' the middle sister chimed in quickly, 'just someone who wasn't quite so—'

'Quite so what, Diana?'

Zoe was still smiling, but only with her mouth.

'I mean,' Di said, 'you've always been a little on the wild side, haven't you?'

Her mother stepped in. 'Di and Cynthia are just curious, Zoe, they don't mean—'

'No, Mom, they're exactly right,' Zoe said, and her voice was bright again. 'Excuse me, I've got to talk to the undertaker about the funeral I arranged.'

She turned and walked back down the aisle. Nick went after her.

'Are you all right?' he asked softly, touching her velvet-covered arm.

'I'm fine.'

He stopped her with more pressure on her arm. 'Zoe, they shouldn't have been speaking to you like that. They might be hurt by your great-aunt's will, but that's no excuse to criticise you.'

'It's nothing new, Nick. Look at them.' She gestured to where the Drakes were talking among themselves, shaking their heads. 'My family is good-looking, successful, married. I'm the one who's a failure; I always have been. Don't let it bother you; it doesn't bother me.'

'I think that's a lie.'

For a moment her blue eyes met his and he could see the pain. Then she was shaking her head and putting on her wide grin.

'Like I always say, the best revenge is not to care. And besides, we know they didn't know Aunt Xenia as well as we do.'

She winked at him, her bravado back in place. 'Anyway, this isn't finding you your father, and the guests are starting to arrive now. If you sit in the back, there, you should be able to see everyone who comes in.'

And that was a dismissal if he'd ever heard one. 'Zoe, this

funeral is going to be difficult enough for you without you and your family winding each other up.'

'Leave my family to me, Nick,' she said firmly. 'You concentrate on yours, okay? Besides, you'd better get your hand off me or everyone will really start thinking you're after me for my money.'

This time he took the hint. He stopped touching her and went to stand near the entrance to the side chapel, where he would be able to see every person coming to the funeral. Guests entered in pairs, groups, singly, talking softly among themselves. They appeared to be from all walks of life. Several women wore elaborate designer outfits, but there were also plainer clothes, work uniforms underneath sombre overcoats, jeans and construction boots. Xenia apparently had made friends with everyone from her local fast-food workers to the cream of Manhattan society.

And yet as he searched faces, glanced at hands, he was thinking about Zoe and her family.

Even as an outsider, even from that short interaction, he could see the Drake family dynamic. Zoe didn't fit in and probably never had. But her family was trying in their own way—maybe not all her sisters, but her parents. Her mother tried to give her compliments and to talk with her about clothes, as she probably did easily with her other, fashion-conscious daughters. Her father was being protective of her, especially where another man was concerned.

But Zoe didn't hear their concern; she heard their implicit criticism of her appearance, her choices, her life. And her way of defending herself against them was to confirm their worst suspicions, turn her pain into a wisecrack.

Her family hurt because she seemed to rebuff their love; Zoe hurt because their love seemed a cover-up for their disappointment.

The crowd had assembled; John took the pulpit and began to speak. Nick drew in a deep lily-scented breath and chose a chair stationed at the back, turning it slightly towards the entrance so he could see any latecomers.

He supposed his own background made him particularly sensitive to how families could operate according to their own strange contradictions. He loved his mother and his sister with a fierce loyalty that sometimes hurt. Yet both he and Kitty had left home as soon as they could, to pursue their own careers. Kitty had gone to California to become an interior designer, and he'd gone off to college to study conservation and spent months at a time in the wilderness as part of his ranger training.

Scanning the crowd for a familiar figure, he wondered if his father had been caught in a similar contradiction as he had. As Zoe was.

His letter hadn't explained anything. It had been three handwritten lines on plain white paper.

Dear Nick, I hope you're doing all right. I heard you got a good job and I hope you are happy. I am fine.
Love, Dad.

The letter was just as mysterious as his disappearance, and both of them made a mockery of the word 'love' at the end.

He looked towards the front of the chapel, where Zoe was sitting at the end of a line of chairs, next to her family. From this angle he couldn't see her face, only the back of her head and her shoulders. Next to her in a line, her mother and her sisters all had long blonde hair, falling down their backs in a golden sheen. Zoe's was short, tousled, tucked behind her ears. It was just as golden, though.

Zoe leaned forward in her chair; even from the back he could tell she was listening intently as John talked about her great-aunt's life. She nodded at his words. Nick knew she was smiling.

Among the complicated negotiations of love and pain, Zoe's emotions for her great-aunt were straightforward. Nick smiled himself, and scanned the crowd again.

He wasn't going to turn up.

Nick took a sip of whiskey in resignation. In fact, the whiskey itself was an acknowledgement that he'd given up the search for the day. He rarely drank more than a beer or two, and never hard liquor; he valued having sharp senses. But a waiter had walked by with glasses of amber liquid and he'd taken one, thinking maybe the alcohol would loosen his shoulders, soothe his nerves made ragged by too much adrenaline.

The funeral had gone on for ages, and then there was the burial and the reception, and in between them the car rides in the long black limousines, from the church to the graveyard, and the graveyard to the hotel. Both times Nick had slipped inside a limo with a group of strangers and listened to their conversation, hoping to catch a word about an Eric Giroux.

On the way to the graveyard he was with a group of poets and artists who had never heard of his father but were fascinated by the quality of the light in Maine, whatever that meant; on the way to the hotel he was with a group of French and Portuguese women who had cleaned Xenia's house over the years. When he mentioned the name Giroux they launched into an animated discussion about a cultural critic and university lecturer who'd written a book on terrorism. Not his father, obviously.

Here at the reception, hosted in a grand room of a hotel whose name even country-boy Nick recognised as a synonym for elegance and sophistication, he hadn't had much better luck. He'd developed a procedure whenever he spotted a man who could just possibly be his father: he hung back, watching, cataloguing physical attributes. A couple of times, even though he hadn't been hit by any recognition, he approached the man and listened in to his conversation, trying to find something in the voice that struck a chord.

Nothing. Not yet, anyway.

Nick took another sip of whiskey and leaned against a gilt-trimmed wall. Of their own accord, his eyes sought out Zoe. He knew exactly where she was already; all day he'd known. He hadn't even had to look for her. It was as if the sixth sense he'd expected would lead him to his father was making him aware of her instead.

She was talking with a group of people, laughing about something. Whenever he'd overheard her conversation today she'd been talking about her great-aunt Xenia, with her big smile on her face. The funeral might have been a sad event for some people; not for Zoe. She seemed determined to celebrate Xenia's life rather than to mourn its passing.

Nick smiled himself, and that relaxed his nerves more than the whiskey had. He straightened and walked across the room, where there was a table for empty glasses. He was just putting his mostly full glass on the table when he heard a female voice, lowered to a near-whisper.

'Yes, but why is she smiling so much?'

'Wouldn't you if you were worth fifty million dollars?'

Nick quietly laid down his drink and turned towards the voices. Two women were standing on the other side of one of the huge flower arrangements. He couldn't see their faces, and he didn't suppose they could see him, but from the glimpses of their clothes he recognised two of Zoe's sisters.

'Cindy, don't be so horrible.'

'I'm not being horrible; it's the truth. Look at her, Di. She's acting like it's a party, not a funeral. She was less cheerful at your *wedding*.'

'You have a point there.'

'All I'm saying is, I think she knew beforehand that she was going to get all the money. Why else did she always hang around Aunt Xenia? Why did she make sure she was the one to arrange the funeral? I wish she'd just tell us and stop pretending it was all such a big surprise. It's typical Zoe.'

Nick's hand clenched into a fist. He strode around the flower arrangement to confront the two surprised women.

'You're being unfair to your sister,' he told them, his voice sounding harsh to his own ears. 'Your great-aunt asked Zoe to arrange the funeral. And she doesn't care about the money; she's not even going to give up driving a cab. I'm a stranger and even I could see within ten minutes of meeting Zoe that she loved her great-aunt. You're her family. Give her a chance.'

Di's eyes were wide and she opened her mouth to answer Nick. But before she could say anything Nick felt a strong hand close around his wrist and he was being hauled backwards away from the two women.

It was Zoe, and her smile had definitely disappeared. 'Excuse us,' she said grimly to her sisters, and pulled harder at Nick's arm.

He let her drag him out of the big room through a door and into a corridor. Immediately they got there she let his arm go and whirled to face him, her face furious.

'What the hell were you doing?' she snarled.

His heart was pounding with anticipation, frustration, anger, and Zoe standing in front of him with her eyes sparking and her cheeks flushed.

'What did it look like I was doing? I was standing up for you.'

'I don't need you to stand up for me.'

'I don't think you heard what your sisters were saying.'

'It doesn't matter what they were saying!' She nearly shouted it, her voice hoarse. 'I don't need you to rescue me, I don't want you to rescue me! I'm not some pathetic animal that needs you to help it! I can take care of myself.'

Her rage was so great that he took a breath, ran his hands through his hair, calmed his voice. 'Zoe, I know you can take care of yourself, but I couldn't keep quiet. They're your family, they should be supportive of you, not—'

'How many times do I need to tell you that I *do not care?*'

The last three words were a shout, and her face was so livid but her eyes were so full of pain, just at that moment telling the completely opposite story to her words, and Nick only saw one way out of this.

He stepped forward and took her face between his hands, swiftly tilted her head up, and kissed her.

Her mouth. Oh, Lord, her mouth. It was warm and lush and soft. He slid one hand up into her hair and put the other on her hip to pull her closer to him, and he kissed her harder.

Zoe made some sort of sound in her throat and he felt her lips move under his. He wasn't sure if it was an invitation but he took it anyway, opening his own mouth and letting his tongue taste her. Her lips were slightly open and he touched the satin heat of the inside of her lip, the smooth ivory of her teeth. He could feel her breasts against his chest and her lean hip fitting into his palm. And her smell, clean and feminine and one hundred per cent Zoe…the hammering of her heart next to his…

He needed more. Nick angled his head, trying to coax her lips open for him, tightening his hands on her, wanting her wrapped around him, pressed as intimately as she could be.

He felt her hands come up to his chest and he nearly groaned, anticipating her fingers on the buttons of his shirt, opening it, stroking his skin.

She pushed at him. Hard.

Surprised, Nick raised his head from hers and looked into her face. Her mouth was red from his kiss, well formed and beautiful and set into a hard line. The pupils of her eyes were dilated, dark against the blue of her irises, but her eyes themselves were narrowed.

She pushed at him again, this time nearly hard enough to bruise him. 'Let me go,' she said, and her voice was strangled, rough and upset.

He loosed his hold on her and she stumbled backwards. Her normal ease in movement seemed to have deserted her; she teetered on her heels. Nick reached out to steady her, but she retreated even more.

'Zoe—'

She breathed harsh and fast. So did he. She wiped the back of her hand against her mouth, as if she were trying to wipe away his kiss.

'I don't need your pity,' she said, and ran past him out the door.

CHAPTER EIGHT

SHE HATED TO admit that Nick was right about anything. But he'd been right about New York. It was noisy.

Zoe sat on the edge of her bed to lace up her sneakers. Her eyes felt full of sand and her body ached and her throat was scratchy and she knew she was fooling herself.

The reason she hadn't slept last night wasn't because it was noisier here in her apartment in the Bronx than in her great-aunt's apartment in Manhattan. She'd lived with the noise for years. The noise hadn't kept her awake; Nick had.

For a couple of seconds she allowed herself to close her eyes and remember. She'd been in his arms. His hand had been in her hair. His body had been big and hot against her. And he'd kissed her, breathtaking and incredible, filling every single cell of her body with delight and longing.

She licked her lip, as if the taste of him could still be there seventeen hours later. It wasn't, but she could taste him in her memory.

He'd been even better than she'd imagined.

Zoe opened her eyes and got to her feet, disgusted with herself.

No, he hadn't been better than she'd imagined. Because in her imagination Nicholas Giroux would have kissed her because he wanted her, because he couldn't resist her, and not because he thought he was some sort of knight in shining armour riding to her rescue. Not because he was a Boy Scout with special badges in lost causes and hopeless quests.

With the thought she pictured him as he'd been yesterday, standing alone, always alone, even in a crowd. Tall and alert, searching every face for his father.

Another wave of longing swept through her, even stronger because it wasn't purely lust.

Right. It was a good thing that she had two back-to-back aerobics classes to teach this morning, because she could do with the endorphins. Plus maybe if she totally exhausted herself she'd be able to come back here and sleep for a couple of hours without being tormented by memories of the best kiss she'd ever had in her life.

Stupid girl. She didn't need to be tormented by the thought of Nick—she had enough stuff to beat herself up about as it was. One thing Xenia's funeral had shown her was how much her great-aunt had touched other people's lives. There hadn't been a single person in that church or at that reception who didn't have fond memories of Xenia or a story about how she'd helped them out with money, time, or kindness.

Zoe was proud of her great-aunt. But she couldn't help wondering whether anybody could say the same thing about her. How many lives she'd touched. If there were any.

And now she had Xenia's fortune, and none of Xenia's talent for spending it, or for helping people. All she had were her jobs, her apartment in the Bronx, and her independence.

Faced with that truth about herself, it was hardly surprising her choice of torture was to remember Nick's kiss. Every melting, thrilling second of it.

As she walked from her bedroom to her living room, she pulled on a sweatshirt, noticing that her nipples were visible through her sports bra and her Lycra top. She could blame Nick for her imminent case of jogger's nipple, as well as her lack of sleep.

Three things happened while her sweatshirt still covered her head. Somebody knocked on the door, she stepped on something that slipped sideways and made her ankle twist, and she yelled out in pain.

Except when she yelled nothing came out but a small-voiced squeak. She sounded like a mouse wearing a gag.

Zoe sat on the floor and pulled her sweatshirt down.

A quick glance at her foot showed her she'd stepped on one of her high-heeled shoes by mistake, and that her ankle was fine. The pain was already subsiding.

Someone was still knocking at the door.

Just a second, she tried to say, but nothing came out again.

Dammit. She'd lost her voice. On a day when she had two classes to teach.

Zoe hauled herself to her feet. She'd have to cancel the classes, which sucked because she looked forward to them and she doubted the community centre would be able to find someone to fill in on such short notice. She tried coughing, but that didn't seem to help. She'd had a tickly throat yesterday, and then she'd talked all day with people at the funeral, and then she hadn't slept. Equalled no voice. It happened to her often when she caught a cold, as if her body was taking away her best defence when a virus took over.

She hoped Nick had caught her germs.

Someone was still knocking at the door. Zoe exhaled in annoyance and opened it.

It was Nick.

How did he get more gorgeous with every passing hour? His hair was wet and curling, he had dark stubble on his chin, and he smelled of rain. Zoe caught her breath, came to her senses, and tried to close the door.

He put his foot between the door and the jamb, and got his shoulder in there, too. 'Zoe, please let me in,' he said.

'How did you find me?' she whispered between gritted teeth. She hadn't been able to face going back to Xenia's apartment yesterday; instead she'd come straight back to the Bronx. She'd known Ralph would let Nick into the apartment after the reception. She'd figured with any luck he'd find his father, and then pack up himself and his pigeon and get the hell out of her life at last.

'If I can track a deer through the woods, I can find you in the Bronx,' he said. 'Can I come in?'

She pushed at the door, but he was too solid. She rolled her eyes and let him in.

Xenia's apartment was big. Zoe's apartment was small. Nick seemed to fill it up with his broad shoulders and his strong body and his big hands, especially since he started talking right away.

'Listen,' he said, 'I don't pity you. I wouldn't dare to pity you. And I didn't mean to upset you, but I'm not sorry I kissed you, and I'm not sorry I defended you, either.'

Where's your white charger, Sir Nicholas? she tried to say, but nothing came out but the now-familiar squeak.

'I was going to come after you right away, but I figured you needed some space to calm down so I went back to the apartment and waited for you. I sat on that damn couch all night waiting for you to turn up. And I know you're a grown woman and I know you live in New York but I was worried about you and you're lucky I didn't turn up here at 3:00 a.m. to make sure you were all right. I was on my way at 3:00 a.m, as a matter of fact, but I figured you'd probably assault me.'

He stopped, and looked at her. 'Why aren't you interrupting me?'

She opened her mouth. *Squeak.*

The corner of his mouth twitched. 'Have you lost your voice?'

Zoe nodded, grudgingly.

'Ha!' Nick threw his head back and slapped his thigh. 'Zoe Drake has lost her voice and can't tell me to shut up!' He sat on her couch, a look of huge enjoyment on his face. 'I think this is my lucky day.'

Zoe glared at him, her hands on her hips. She stomped into the kitchen and got down the whiteboard and pen she used to write herself notes. She rubbed off a shopping list with her cuff as she went back to the living room, and then wrote on the board and held it up for Nick to see.

'You are incredibly annoying.'

He laughed. 'Does this mean you haven't calmed down since yesterday?'

She rubbed and scribbled. 'Forget 3:00 a.m., you're in danger of being assaulted right now.'

He didn't seem bothered by the threat. He looked around her living room, bare and functional as usual, tidy except for her shoes on the floor. 'Where's all your stuff?'

She furrowed her brow in an obvious question.

'You know. All your clothes and handbags and fashion magazines and all that other stuff women always have all over their houses.'

Don't be stupid, her look said. He nodded, seemingly in approval.

'Fine. Listen. I want you to know that I kissed you because I'm attracted to you. Plain and simple.'

For a minute, she almost believed it.

Plain and simple. He wanted her as she wanted him. She had lightning-fast visions of joining him on the couch, sinking her fingers into his damp, curling hair, and kissing him back as hard as she'd wanted to yesterday. Pulling his T-shirt over his head and seeing his bare chest, close up this time.

'And you looked like you needed to be kissed,' he added.

The visions vanished. She remembered being close in his arms, and him yawning. She remembered how he took off his clothes in her presence as if he hadn't noticed she was a red-blooded female. She remembered the damn pigeon.

She'd needed to be kissed.

It was just another rescue mission.

'In fact, I'd really like to do it again. But only if you're interested.'

Do it again? If she was interested? The visions of kissing him and stripping him came stampeding back into her brain and she had to grit her teeth not to throw herself onto the couch and plaster herself all over him.

She needed to think of something, and fast, before she let herself become the charity case she'd sworn never to be.

And then she thought of something.

She rubbed off what she'd written on the board and wrote rapidly, concentrating on the words rather than him sitting there, big and male and gorgeous and inviting her to kiss him. She finished and turned the board to face him.

'Okay, lover-boy, if you're so hot to help me out, I've got something you can do for me.'

Nick, reading, raised his eyebrows.

'I'd be happy to,' he said, and his voice made her think of bedrooms, caresses, sweat.

'Good,' she wrote. 'Let's go. We don't have much time, and you need a pair of sneakers.'

Nick watched as Zoe placed a brightly coloured plastic box in front of him on the polished gym floor.

'What's this?' he asked.

A step, she mouthed. She demonstrated by climbing onto it with her sneaker-clad feet, and then stepping back off.

'What am I supposed to do with it?'

She gestured at the sheet of instructions she'd written out for him on the subway to Manhattan and while he was changing into clothes he could exercise in.

The first class is step aerobics, and the second is a toning class. All you have to do is follow along, do the exercises with me, and when I nod at you, call out what I've written on this sheet so everyone knows what's coming next.

'You call this exercise? Stepping up and down on a plastic box?'

She just looked at him. There was a glint in her eye that he wasn't sure was good for him. It was pretty incredible, how she could communicate without any words.

And she could let her body talk to him any time she wanted to, he thought. She was wearing Lycra shorts that showed off her perfect hips and backside, and her beautiful toned legs were completely bare. When they'd reached the midtown gym she'd taken off her big sweatshirt to reveal a tight sleeveless top. The whole outfit didn't leave much to the imagination, although his imagination was working overtime anyway.

Nick was wearing a T-shirt and shorts and if he studied Zoe any more his arousal was going to be obvious to the entire class, who were starting to come into the room. He watched the plastic box instead as he moved it around with his foot.

'I guess in New York you don't have mountains to climb or trees to cut down,' Nick said, trying to distract himself. 'Plastic boxes are probably the best you can do.'

Zoe snorted and went back to sorting through CDs. The students were mostly women, Nick noticed, all of them fit-looking, though nothing compared to Zoe. All of them greeted Zoe as they came through, and gave Nick the once-over.

Nick didn't mind being in rooms full of women. He liked women. Still, he was relieved to see a few men among the people setting up steps. He'd never been much of a gym person; even in the winter he preferred to exercise outdoors, cross-country skiing or snowshoeing. He didn't think he'd ever been in a room like this, a dance studio with mirrored walls and full-length windows looking out at the Manhattan street below. The men made him feel a little bit less as if he were in an alien world. He smiled and nodded at them.

Zoe signalled the start of the class by putting on music, a high-energy dance track, and taking her place at the front of the room. Without a word from her or him the class fell into step together, jogging in place behind their steps.

Nick was situated at the front of the room, diagonally to Zoe so he could watch her, and so that the class could hear him. He started jogging in place, too. Although he doubted he'd get much of a workout, he might as well make the most of it since he was here; he'd been cooped up so long in the city that his muscles could use some action.

Plus, if he was lucky, it would tire him out enough so that he'd have a little bit less sexual energy. He seemed to like Zoe better and better in every outfit he saw her in, and he was spending a whole lot of time thinking about her in no outfit at all.

Zoe nodded at him and he read off the sheet he held in his hand. 'Twenty basic, right foot,' he said, and immediately the class began to step in time onto their boxes and off again.

What a weird way to exercise. There were hundreds of skyscrapers; surely New Yorkers could climb up and down steps whenever they wanted to.

There was a plus to this kind of exercise, though. He watched Zoe step energetically up onto her box, and then back down again. The action tensed her thigh and calf muscles, and the movement made her breasts bounce under her snug top. Nick moved up and down to the rhythm of the music, unable to take his gaze away from the tantalising rhythm Zoe's body was creating.

She clapped her hands, and Nick blinked. He raised his eyes from her chest to her face and saw her nodding at him.

'Oh.' He looked down at the paper he held. 'Twenty basic, left foot.'

The class switched feet without missing a beat. Nick had to think about it, but within seconds he was stepping with his left foot and doing his best not to let himself stare at Zoe's chest again. He tried looking past her, but the mirror behind her gave a perfect view of her buttocks flexing and tightening.

Hell. Imagine her walking up the stairs in front of him. On their way to a bedroom. Her backside at eye level. Imagine sliding his hand over her curves, down over the swell of one buttock and around her firm thigh.

Zoe clapped again and he nearly stumbled as he held up the paper. 'Three knee-lift repeater,' he read, and, though that made absolutely no sense, the rest of the class immediately stepped up onto their boxes in time and lifted their knees three times in a row.

Yeah. He could do this. He stepped up and lifted his knee and then saw that the rest of the class had moved to the other side of their steps and were doing the same thing with the other leg. By the time he got to the other side of the step, the class was going back to their first position.

He looked at Zoe. She was grinning like a madwoman, and her breasts were still moving in that wonderful way. When she lifted her knee he could see the inside of her thigh.

Nick missed the step completely and landed hard on the floor, jolting his ankle.

He scrambled to get back into the rhythm of the exercise, but as soon as he'd lifted his knee again he heard Zoe clapping, and had to read out the next instruction. And then the next. And the next, all of which seemed to be in a code everyone but him understood.

This wasn't easy. This was torture.

Nick had to watch his feet because if he didn't, he'd fall off the step again, but if he didn't watch Zoe, he'd miss his cue. But if he watched Zoe, he looked at her body moving and he thought more and more about her body moving with his, the athleticism she'd take to sex, and the minute he thought about that he felt his penis hardening and then he stumbled even more. Sweat dripped from him; he had to blink it out of his eyes and that made everything even worse.

'Around the world,' he gasped to Zoe's nod. Everybody skipped over their step, arms circling, and Nick groaned. The music was building to a climax. Nick watched Zoe launching herself into the air and wished he were building to a climax, too.

It seemed to last a muscle-burning, ankle-twisting, arousing eternity before the music finally slowed and the exercise pace calmed, back to easy steps and finally to stretches. Nick saw on the sheet, incredulously, that this section of the class was called the 'cooldown'.

Zoe stretched forward, her long leg extended behind her along with her arms, a posture that thrust her breasts forward towards him. Her nipples were erect underneath her shirt and sports bra. She seemed to be sweating a whole lot less than he was, but her face and neck gleamed. He imagined the taste of salty moisture on her skin.

This wasn't even remotely like a cooldown.

The end of the CD and applause from the class told him the session had finished. He mopped sweat off his forehead with the bottom of his T-shirt and silently thanked God.

'How'd you like that?' It was a male voice with a heavy New York accent.

Nick pulled his shirt down off his face. 'It was pure hell,' he said to the person who'd spoken to him, one of the guys he'd smiled at in solidarity at the beginning of the lesson.

The guy laughed. 'Zoe's great, ain't she? You not used to this kind of workout?'

'I'm not used to anything in New York.'

'What kind of workout you usually do?'

'Chasing animals, lifting rocks, that sort of thing.' He filled a cup from the water cooler at the front of the room and drained it in one gulp.

'You interested in going for coffee?' the guy asked.

Nick, mid-gulp of his second cup of water, noticed for the first time that the guy was looking at him with more appreciation than friendliness.

'Thanks,' he said, 'but I'm not around for long.'

The guy shrugged. 'No harm in asking. See ya.'

As he moved away Nick saw another person, this one female and brunette, approach him. 'Since you didn't say yes to Carl,' she said, smiling, 'how about coffee with me?'

'Uh. Thanks. But as I said to Carl—'

'You're not around for long.' The brunette's eyes darted to Zoe, and she smiled knowingly. 'Sure. Have a good time.'

Nick let out a long breath as Zoe came over. Her smile was devilish, and her eyes sparkled. She wasn't winded at all from the exercise.

'New York is crazy,' he said in answer to her raised eyebrows. 'I've never turned down two dates in two minutes before.'

She pressed her lips together as if she were stifling a laugh, and handed him another sheet of paper. Then she picked up a pair of dumb-bells from a container on the floor and gave them to him. Three minutes till the next class, she mouthed, and went back to her CDs.

Nick sank down on the plastic step, wiped his face again, and wished he were in the woods.

'That's it, folks.'

Zoe heard more than a note of relief in Nick's voice.

Surreptitiously, she watched him as he returned his gym mat and dumb-bells to the boxes at the front of the room.

He was fit. Very fit. His shorts revealed legs roped with muscle, and whenever she'd caught a glimpse of him lifting a weight she'd just about gasped. He wasn't used to gym exercise, because he didn't know any of the moves and he had to work out twice as hard as everyone else in the room to get it right and then keep up. Still, he hadn't stopped. His T-shirt was soaked with sweat in deep Vs on his front and his back, in a way that Zoe found distractingly sexy, but he wasn't puffed.

Zoe packed away her own CDs and her own mat and smiled to herself. He hadn't enjoyed it. Whenever she'd glanced at his face, he'd looked as if he were trying out that thumbscrew collection on Xenia's wall. But he hadn't complained, and he hadn't given up. He hadn't really had to do every exercise, but he had done. And he'd followed her instructions to the letter.

It was just the kind of damn noble guy he was.

'Bye, Zoe!' said the last of her class as they left, and Zoe waved at them from her crouching position on the floor. She heard the door shut and then she knew without even looking around that she and Nick were alone, because the room seemed hotter and paradoxically smaller.

'Well, that was fun,' Nick said, from over near the door, and she heard him walking closer. She concentrated on zipping up her gym bag. Exercise always warmed her blood, made her feel good. Made her feel sexy. And that was dangerous with Nick around.

You hated it, she mouthed, and he laughed.

'It was different from the stuff I normally do, but then again, everything's different in New York.' He was standing right next to her, and she could see his strong, hair-roughened calves. She thought about his shorts; they covered him, but there wasn't a whole lot of spare material. She turned away and began fiddling unnecessarily with the CD player, just to give herself a few minutes to calm down before she looked him in the eye.

'We need to talk,' Nick said. She did look up at him then, and pointed at her throat.

'Okay, I need to talk, and you need to listen, because I'm desperate here. We didn't finish our conversation this morning. About why I kissed you. About how attracted I am to you.'

Her heart had slowed down after the exercise; now it began to race.

She stood and shook her head, waving her hand in a dismissive way. Of course standing up meant that she was closer to him, close enough to touch. Close enough to smell clean sweat and the cotton of his T-shirt. Close enough to see the stubble on his chin and the darkness of his eyes and to feel the heat of his body.

'Are you shaking your head because you're not attracted to me, or because you don't believe that I'm attracted to you?'

How the hell was she supposed to answer that? Especially with no voice? She swallowed.

'Let me make it simpler. Are you attracted to me?'

Lord, he was so close and she couldn't possibly think. Zoe retreated a step and felt her back pressing against the mirrored wall behind her. Nick stepped forward. His face was too intense, his eyes too dark and deep.

She should make a smart answer. She should protect herself. She couldn't.

She dipped her gaze to escape and found herself staring at the base of his neck where his T-shirt met his skin. There were a few strands of curling hair. She could see his pulse beating strong.

Zoe licked her lips, imagining despite herself the taste of his skin.

'That's the answer I wanted,' Nick said, his voice soft and low, and he leaned forward, each arm braced on the mirror behind her, and kissed her.

This man's mouth was perfect along with everything else about him and now that he was touching her Zoe officially lost her mind.

She kissed him back.

CHAPTER NINE

SHE WAS GREEDY, greedy, and she opened her mouth to him and kissed him as if she were devouring him. Nick made a sound of surprise and pleasure in his throat and that made her hungrier. Her tongue swept against his, feeling the strength in his kiss, the smooth hardness of his teeth.

She pressed her hands against the mirror behind her, curling her fingers on the glass. She wanted to touch him, not just with her mouth but with her hands and her whole body, but the wanting was too powerful, just with touching his lips with her own. It would take her over.

But his kiss, dear God, it was perfect. He began gentle and then responded to her own ferocity. She took all she could, bit his lip and smoothed it with the tip of her tongue, let her sense of taste and smell be overwhelmed by him, the rasp of his stubble on her chin, the saltiness of sweat on his upper lip.

Nick, she thought, *I can even taste how kind you are.*

When he broke from her they were both panting raggedly. He only moved his face a fraction from hers and she could feel his breath hot on her wet lips.

'Do you believe I'm attracted to you now?' he asked.

She hesitated.

'And before you make some crack about me having just come out of the woods and being desperate for any woman, let me remind you that I'm in the biggest city in America and I've just said no to a woman and a man. It's you I want.'

She'd dreamed about these words. She looked into his dark eyes, trying to judge if he was telling the truth.

It hadn't been the truth before, not on their first night together. But maybe something had changed. She'd wanted Nick instantly, but maybe his attraction for her had come later. Grown. Did that make it less genuine, or more?

'I kept on falling off the box during your class because I was concentrating so hard on not watching your body because I knew it would turn me on. And these shorts don't conceal much.'

She looked down, and all the air rushed out of her lungs.

His shorts didn't conceal anything. His erection tented the front, straining the material in a long, thick line. She could easily imagine its length, its girth, how it would feel in her hands, stone in velvet skin, hot and alive.

Screw her doubts about why he wanted her. He did. And she wanted him, more than she could remember wanting anything in a very long time.

Zoe uncurled her hands and lifted them to his chest. She touched the damp material of his T-shirt and felt the firmness of his muscles underneath. It seemed as if she'd looked at him a million times, wanting to touch him, although some of those times must have been in dreams. He felt better than she could have possibly imagined. The solid curve of his collar-bone, his pecs, his nipples just tangible through the T-shirt. The beating of his heart. The sound of his breathing, how it caught in his throat as her hands trailed down his front, over his hard abs, and then underneath his shirt to touch his skin.

She wanted to savour touching his stomach, the bare, warm skin, the soft hair around his navel, but Nick grasped her in his arms and pulled her closer, his mouth meeting hers again. This kiss didn't start gentle. This kiss started carnal, and Nick's hands were everywhere—her hips, her waist, her back, in her hair, one suddenly and wonderfully on her breast. Zoe dug her fingertips into Nick's skin and arched closer to him. His erection pressed hard against her belly and she heard him groan.

'Zoe, you are so sexy,' he muttered roughly into her mouth and she let out a voiceless sigh of pleasure in return as he cupped his hand around her breast and stroked her nipple with his thumb. His big, strong body leaned forward, pinning her against the mirrored wall, the two of them touching from head to toe.

His mouth left hers and Zoe leaned her head back against the wall as he dropped hot kisses over her face and throat. She felt his tongue tasting her skin, and shuddered.

'You're beautiful,' he murmured, and he was so ardent and turned on and he filled her world so much that she believed him. She was carried away into his emotions, into his view of things.

She felt beautiful. It was a glow, a lift, a rush of desire that was stronger and more immediate than any feeling she'd ever had before.

Zoe's hands stopped moving on Nick's skin as she realised it was also the most dangerous. She loved this feeling. She'd been craving it for far too long.

If she made love with this man, she would be his. She would belong to him, body and soul.

Zoe pulled her hands from underneath Nick's T-shirt and put them on his shoulders. Then she pushed him away.

'Stop,' she panted, and wasn't at all surprised that this was the moment her voice chose to come back.

The moment she'd decided to mess everything up.

Nick didn't step away; she was strong, but he was solid and a lot stronger. His body still pressed against hers, every breath going through her, too. But he raised his head and looked into her face.

'Zoe?' His pupils were dilated, his brows drawn together in concern, his mouth moist and beautiful. She wanted to take his face between her palms, let the stubble tickle her, and kiss him.

Instead she pushed again. 'Nick, cut it out.' Her voice was rough and croaky.

He took his hand away from her breast and straightened, steadying her with the other hand but not touching her otherwise. Typical white knight, obeying her requests, she thought, while her body ached to have him back again.

'What's the matter?' he asked.

'I—' *I don't want to fall in love with you.* She couldn't say that. 'Didn't you just tell those two people that you were leaving soon?'

'Yeah, but that was because I wasn't interested in them. I am interested in you.'

'But you're still leaving.'

The concern in his eyes hardened a little, and Zoe saw it. The chink in his shining armour. How she could push him away so he'd really go.

'I mean, come on, Nick, you hate New York. You're not staying around here any longer than you have to, right?'

He looked as if he wanted to say something; he opened his mouth. But then he closed it again, his expression unsure, and Zoe pressed forward, using the chink to make herself safe.

'Isn't that what you hate about your father?' she said. 'The fact that he left?'

Nick stepped back from her. His eyes narrowed and he stood tall, his jaw clenched, his fists bunched.

'If that's how you feel I'll go back with you to the apartment and pack my stuff,' he said.

On his way to the door he grabbed the paper cup he'd been drinking from and flung it into the garbage can so hard it made a clang.

Zoe glanced at the mirror on her way out. The outline of her body, pressed in steam against the glass, pressed there by Nick, was just fading away.

Nicholas Giroux furious was like a powerful storm cloud, waiting to break. It was the dark opposite of his passion.

As they neared the apartment door Zoe remembered the first time she'd seen him, standing on this spot towering with rage against his missing father. That anger was directed at her now. She could feel it, a heat that was seductive, somehow, because it was so immediate and strong.

And because it was totally justified. She'd just said something that was, in his world, unforgivable. Because she'd panicked.

But his anger was safer than his passion. She reminded herself of that as she opened the door for him and watched him go straight into the small guest room to pack his bag. Knowing him, everything was packed away already; the man was scrupulously tidy about not leaving traces of himself everywhere.

She wondered if it had been trained into him by his profession, or whether it was something deeper than that, something that came from being abandoned as a kid. An apology to the world for being unhappy, wanting more than he had, an effort to keep everything where it belonged, even if that everything couldn't include his father.

The thought twisted her stomach in pain.

I'm sorry, she thought at him.

'You going to take that pigeon with you, too?' she said, leaning against the doorway into the guest room, pretending she didn't care that he was going, or that she had hurt him.

'Don't worry,' he said grimly. 'I'll take him away. You won't be forced to have any responsibility or care about anything once I'm gone.'

It was so close to what she'd been thinking that her eyes narrowed.

'Tell me about this whole responsibility thing, Nick. I'm genuinely interested. You've come down to New York to rub your father's neglected duties in his face, and you thought while you were at it that you'd have a little fun sex with me? Just to show what an upright, caring guy you are?'

He straightened from packing his bag. 'At first I decided not to touch you, Zoe,' he said quietly. 'I don't have flings or one-night stands. I've stayed away from women for a long time because my job takes me away from people for weeks on end. I won't commit and then leave somebody. I won't.'

The vehemence in his voice burnt her heart.

'But I wanted you,' he continued, his voice still quiet, but rough with honesty. 'If it were just about your body, I could've kept on resisting it. But it's not. You can deny it all you want, but there's something inside you that wants human contact more than anything else. It's so attractive to me that I can't stand it.'

Zoe nearly staggered backwards.

Oh, God, she'd been right. He knew her, he saw her already. She forced herself to put on a sceptical smile, to raise her eyebrows.

'They teach you mind-reading along with bird first-aid at ranger school, Boy Scout?'

He shoved his toiletry bag into his backpack, more roughly then necessary, and then zipped the pack up with short, quick tugs.

'I shouldn't have touched you. I'm going away and I can't offer you anything. But I am not like my father, Zoe.' He said the words slowly, holding her gaze with his own. 'I'm not.'

Zoe knew all about denial. She recognised it like an old, half-unwelcome friend. She knew how it made you too vehement, how it made you insist too much because you wanted to convince yourself, because if you didn't face the truth, if you didn't admit that you cared, life was easier.

Recognising it in Nick made her stomach twist even more, with the realisation of just how much she did care. About him. And how much she didn't want him to go away.

So of course she chose her next words to drive him away even faster.

'Sure, you're not like him,' she said. 'You take care of things. You save lost causes. You do everything you can do to show that you're not like your father at all. So why do you need to prove it, Nick? Unless you think that really, down deep, you're exactly like him?'

Nick's dark eyes snapped. 'Let's talk about your family, Zoe. Because you haven't met my father, but I've met yours, and your mother. They love you, you know. They might not be great at showing it, but they do. And all you do to them is push them away with both hands.' He swung his pack onto his back. 'I don't think you're one to talk about family.'

We're arguing about everything except what we feel about each other, she thought. But that was fine. Because she didn't plan to show him what she felt about him, not in a million years.

'That's funny,' she said, 'I thought you were all hot on my

108 HIS FOR THE TAKING

family not being fair to me. Or maybe that was just an excuse for you, so you'd have some bad guys to defend me from. So you could get rewarded with a grateful kiss.'

'Zoe, I kissed you because I wanted to. I still want to now, even though you're doing your best to piss me off.' He walked to the door of the room, where she still leant against the post, blocking the way through. 'Are you going to let me through, or do I have to resort to kissing again?'

Him so close brought back full-body memories of him pressed against her in the gym. If she touched him again, within jumping distance of a bed, she wouldn't stop until both of them were naked and sated.

She stepped aside, and he walked past.

She followed him. She couldn't help it. It was as if he had attached a string to her guts and was leading her around the apartment like a pathetic little puppy. They went into the living room and he gently picked up the box with the pigeon in it and tucked it underneath his arm. He'd cut some air holes in it, she saw, and wired up a drinking bottle to the side. It was practically the pigeon equivalent of an upper west side Manhattan apartment.

She remembered him searching the apartment for his father. Laughing with her on the couch, sharing pizza.

Don't go.

She followed him down the hallway to the door, where he stopped.

'Well,' he said. 'Thanks for everything, Zoe. Thanks for trying to help me find my father. Take care of yourself.'

She nodded, unable to look at his face. He lifted his left hand, as if he was going to touch her with it, and then dropped it again. He opened the door and went out.

Yeah. Take care of herself. That was what she did best. That was what she was doing now.

And when the door shut behind him she felt as if her guts were being cut in half and dragged out with him.

She ran to the living room window. It looked out onto the street; she would be able to see him when he emerged from the building. Zoe didn't think about what the purpose of watching him walk away from her would be. She only knew she wanted one last sight of him.

Her phone in her gym bag, still on her shoulder, buzzed and rang and she groped inside her bag, keeping her gaze on the street below. For a crazy minute she thought maybe Nick was calling her, but then she realised of course she'd never given him her number.

She found her phone and glanced at the screen for the split-test of split seconds before staring at the street again. It was Xenia's lawyer. She didn't feel like talking to Xenia's lawyer, but to be honest she could probably do with some distraction right now. She pressed the answer button and put it to her ear.

'Hello, Mr Feinberg,' she said.

The lawyer exchanged pleasantries with her and then started talking about making an appointment to go through Xenia's estate. Zoe answered automatically, not really listening because the sidewalk below was full of people but none of them, yet, was Nick.

'I have Brenda here with my appointment book, and it appears I have Thursday afternoon, if that would be convenient for you. Since the estate is substantial, it will probably take most of the afternoon for us to go through the main part of it.'

'Mmm?' The words were a buzz, a distraction, and she should probably make an excuse and hang up, but Zoe felt as if this calm voice right here were the only thing that was stopping her from running out the door after Nick.

Suddenly, Nick was below her. From up here he should look smaller, but he didn't. He looked like everything she'd ever wanted. She sucked in a sharp breath.

'Miss Drake, are you all right?'

Zoe put one hand on the window-pane and pressed hard against the glass. 'I'm fine, Mr Feinberg. Please, tell me more. You were saying the estate is complicated?'

She didn't hear the next few words he said because Nick was walking away from her. She could barely see his head over the bulk of his backpack, but she saw his arm curled around the pigeon box, his legs in his shorts. And of course she'd memorised the way he moved, even after only five days.

'For example there's a condominium in the Napa Valley, and a house in Maine, and some property on Cape—'

One word, somehow, bit through the longing and loss.

'Maine?' she gasped.

'Pardon me?'

'Xenia had a house in Maine?'

'Yes, in—let me see—'

She couldn't wait. 'I've got to go,' she said, and sprinted for the door.

Someone was just getting out of the elevator when she got to it and she darted inside, hitting the button for the ground floor with the side of the hand that still held her cell phone. The doors slid shut and she paced back and forth in the small box, muttering for it to hurry, hurry, but it didn't, it crawled and creaked and picked up another two passengers going down until finally the door dinged and opened on the ground floor. Zoe slipped past the other passengers and ran through the lobby, out the glass doors and onto the street.

There were too many people in New York, too much *stuff*. Zoe hurtled down the sidewalk, dodging pedestrians, vaulting kerbs. Nick wasn't in sight, wasn't in sight, and then, suddenly, between a hot dog cart and a spindly tree, there he was.

'Nick!' she cried out and reached out and grabbed his warm, perfect, bare arm.

He stopped. He looked surprised to see her, and, she saw with a thump of her heart, he looked pleased, too.

She had to pause to catch her breath before she spoke, not just because of the running but because of nearly losing him. He stood and waited, perfectly still. He looked as if he could stand and wait for ever.

'I just got a phone call from Xenia's lawyer,' she gasped. He didn't move, but his eyes opened slightly wider.

'Xenia had a house in Maine.'

Then, he moved. He tilted his head slightly, thinking. 'You

think she met my father in Maine? I don't even know that he's been in Maine at any time in the past sixteen years.'

True. But that hadn't seemed important when she'd had a reason to talk to Nick again. It didn't seem all that important now, with his gaze on her, with her lungs full of his scent, with his body close enough to touch.

'Well, it seems like a big coincidence to me,' she said.

'Where in Maine?'

'Oh. I don't know. I hung up before he could tell me.' She remembered she was still holding her cell phone, and thumbed the keys to call the lawyer back.

'Saul Feinberg.'

'Mr Feinberg? It's Zoe Drake again. I'm sorry I hung up before. Listen, could you tell me where Xenia's house in Maine is?'

'I can, because I was just looking it up when we last spoke.' The lawyer sounded amused. 'It's in a place called Southwest Harbour.'

'Southwest Harbour,' Zoe told Nick, and Nick's eyebrows went up, and Zoe laughed.

'Thanks,' she told the lawyer, and hung up the phone again.

'Southwest Harbour is on Mount Desert Island,' Nick said. 'Where I work.'

'That's got to mean something, Nick! This is it, this is the link between my great-aunt and your dad!' She felt buoyant, excited. After the torture of forcing him away, the joy of talking to him overwhelmed her.

He nodded. 'Okay. I'll go to Southwest Harbour and ask some questions. Thanks.'

His tone was final, and although he didn't turn away, he was about to, and him leaving was what Zoe had planned all along, but just at that moment she couldn't bear the thought of having her guts snapped again, of looking at his back as he left.

'We'll both go,' she said quickly.

CHAPTER TEN

'YOU'RE COMING WITH me?'

'Of course I am. How do you expect to get into my great-aunt's house without me?'

'How do you expect to get in your great-aunt's house yourself?'

Good question. Zoe pressed the redial button on her phone.

'Saul Feinberg.'

'Mr Feinberg, it's Zoe again. Where's this house in Southwest Harbour and how do I get into it?'

The lawyer laughed for a long time. 'Why don't you come to the office now, Zoe, and we'll sort it out for you.'

'Great.' She hung up, and looked at Nick. He still hadn't moved. She couldn't quite tell what he was thinking. 'We need to go to the lawyer's. I assume he can give me the keys.'

Nick didn't say anything.

'What?' Zoe asked.

'Five minutes ago we were having an argument. And now you say you're coming to Maine with me. It feels like we've skipped a step or two here.'

Yeah, like the step where Zoe stopped and thought about what the hell she was doing throwing herself right back into the fire with Nick.

But she wasn't going to think about that yet. She'd been in pain, and now she wasn't, and that was enough for right now.

'It's no big deal, Nick. I want to see my great-aunt's house.

And I want you to find your father. We can kill two birds with one stone.'

The pigeon chose that moment to start cooing in the box Nick held, and Zoe regretted her metaphor. Nick didn't seem to notice. He was watching her closely.

'Is there anything else you want to do?' he asked.

Zoe drew in a deep breath. She wanted to grab him by the collar of his T-shirt, march him back upstairs to the apartment, and have sex with him until neither of them could move, but that topic was off limits.

And besides, she wanted something more than that. She wanted not to have hurt him.

'Yeah,' she said. 'I apologise for saying you were like your dad. You're not. You're a good guy, Nick. I haven't known you for long, but I know that.'

He nodded. 'Thank you.'

'No problem. Come on, let's go to the lawyer's.'

Nick still didn't shift. 'Don't you think there's something else we should talk about?'

He meant the whole sex-until-neither-of-them-could-move thing. Zoe wasn't going there.

'I'm sorry for kicking out the pigeon, too. Can we go?'

Finally, he smiled. It was as heartlifting as the sun breaking through clouds. 'That'll do for now,' he said, and they started down the sidewalk together.

'You drove all the way down here from Maine in *that*?'

'Sure did.' Nick opened the tailgate of his truck and slid his backpack into the capped-in bed. He held his hand out for Zoe's bag and wasn't surprised when she stepped past him and loaded it in herself.

'Wow, you're braver than I thought.' She stepped back and surveyed his truck, grinning broadly as she took in the mud splashes, the dents, the scratches in the paintwork. 'And I thought New York traffic was murder on cars.'

Nick laughed. Ever since she'd found out about her great-aunt's place in Maine, Zoe had been in an incredibly good mood. She'd been smiling, laughing, joking, teasing him, even whistling as they'd walked from the apartment to the parking garage where he'd left his truck for the past several days. She had a great whistle: tuneful, mellow, the sound of careless cheer.

He wasn't exactly sure why she'd gone from arguing with him to helping him. Or why she'd gone from angry to happy. He did know why she'd picked a fight with him in the first place—as soon as he'd left the apartment building he'd realised that Zoe had been trying to push him away, in exactly the same way he'd seen her use with her family.

Not that that made it any better. He didn't like being pushed away. But it made her apology easy to accept, and it made him glad to see her happy.

'This truck has seen me through mudslides, snowstorms, and washed-out roads,' he said. 'It's been charged by moose twice and it's carried an entire flock of oil-slicked puffins. A little New York traffic ain't nothin'.'

He reached into the back and wrestled out a medium-sized animal carrier. It was big for a pigeon, but it would have to do.

The pigeon tried to dodge his hands when he lifted it out of the cardboard box. It was a good sign. He carefully transferred it into the animal carrier, making sure the floor would be comfortable for its injured feet.

'Will he be okay in there?' To his surprise, Zoe was watching over his shoulder.

'Fine.' He wired up the water bottle. 'This carrier is designed to transport animals.'

'Yeah, but won't the truck bother him? The noise and the shaking and stuff?'

'If it were a loon from the wilds of Oquossoc, I would be worried. This is a New York pigeon. It's lived within inches of traffic all its life. I don't think a cushioned trip in the back of a truck is going to faze it much.' He fastened the door, then shut up the tailgate, and turned to Zoe. 'Anyway, since when do you care about vermin?'

She unfurrowed her brow, removing all expression of concern, and shrugged. 'I'm just being humane, that's all. I mean, I'd hate for all your hard rescue work to be for nothing.'

Nick had to stop himself from hugging her. The tough front, the soft inside. He'd never met anybody like her in his life.

'So, let's get going,' she said, and held out her hand. 'Give me the keys.'

'You want to drive my truck?'

'Yes.'

'I thought you said it was a wreck.'

'That was until I learned it could withstand moose.' She wiggled her fingers, gesturing for the keys.

'You ever driven a truck before?'

Zoe put her hands on her hips. 'Listen, Nick, it's your choice. You want to deal with New York traffic? Or do you want the girl who drives a cab for a living to do it?'

'Good point.' He tossed her the keys. She caught them on her finger and grinned.

'I'll take you on the scenic route,' she said. 'Give you a few good memories of the place.'

Nick watched as she practically skipped to the cab, unlocked the door, and climbed in. She had to step up pretty far, and the movement displayed her legs and bottom to perfection. She looked back at him and winked before she shut the door.

How had this happened? he wondered as he walked around to the passenger door. How had Zoe gone in his perception from just some woman, to a sexy woman, to the sexiest woman he had ever met in his life? So sexy he'd broken his own better judgement and touched her even though he couldn't stay with her? So sexy he was seriously doubting his own ability to sit in the enclosed cab of a truck with her and keep his hands to himself?

She leaned over to unlock the passenger door and he did his best not to stare at her cleavage through the window.

'The clutch is a little bit tricky,' he said to her as he climbed in and buckled his seat belt.

'No problem.' She turned the key in the ignition.

'I mean it—I've fixed it a million times and it still sticks. You've got to—'

'No problem,' she repeated, put the truck in gear, and drove smoothly off down the parking lot ramp.

She was good. He relaxed into his seat and watched her smiling.

'Do you really drive this wreck around everywhere?' she asked. 'How do you ever get girlfriends?'

'I have a Harley for fun. And any girl I was interested in would have to see past the truck to my other fine qualities.'

'Hmm,' Zoe said. Nick paid for the parking and Zoe pulled out into traffic with deft certainty.

'How long have you been driving a cab?' he asked.

'About five years. I'm thinking about cutting it down, doing more on the fitness side. Personal training, some coaching, stuff like that. You have to deal with fewer weirdos.'

She dug a packet of throat lozenges out of the pocket of her sweatshirt and popped one in her mouth. 'Anyway, enough about my job, let's look at New York. On the right is the Dakota, which is where John Lennon lived and was murdered.'

'*Rosemary's Baby* was shot there,' Nick said.

'Yeah, how'd you know that?'

'My sister's husband owns a cinema in Portland. He's obsessed with the movies.' He glanced at the peaked-roofed brick building with its balconies and railings, and then his eyes were drawn back to Zoe. 'You're a great fitness instructor. I mean, I sucked and even I learned something.'

'You weren't that bad.' She gestured through the windshield. 'Here we are in Columbus Circle, coming onto Broadway, and there's a deli down there that does the best pastrami sandwiches you will ever have in your life.'

'Not that bad, huh? Are you talking about the exercising, or the kissing?'

A blush tinged her fair skin. It was incredibly feminine, and Nick couldn't take his eyes off it. 'Exercising. See that doorway?' From the hasty way she spoke, he could tell she was changing the subject deliberately. 'On a cold night, it's

one of the warmest places outside in the neighbourhood. Hot
air vents nearby.'

'Why do you know that?'

'Oh.' She sucked on her lozenge for a moment before she
answered. Nick could see the exact moment she decided to trust
him with an answer.

'I ran away from home when I was sixteen.'

'And you ended up sleeping on the streets of New York?'

'I didn't mean to. I meant to go stay with Xenia, but of course
I didn't call her first and she wasn't at home. So I just hung
around New York for a couple weeks.'

'On your own? At sixteen?' All of his protective instincts
flared up.

'It was an education.' She shot him a crooked smile, and held
out her right hand where she wore a silver ring on her thumb. 'See
this ring? On my second night I found it about a block east of
here, kicked into a corner. I've worn it ever since.'

The ring was battered and scratched, no longer round. Nick had
noticed it before. 'You wanted a reminder of being a runaway?'

'I wanted a reminder of the fact that I can take care of myself.'

Nick pictured Zoe at sixteen, skinny, tough, and vulnerable.
He pictured her curling up in the doorway she'd pointed out to
him, a young kid in faded jeans and sneakers and a jacket that
was too big for her, her golden hair tender and soft against the
rough stone of the building.

He didn't like the picture.

'Why did you run away from home?'

She shrugged. He was beginning to understand that with Zoe the
gesture meant exactly the opposite of what it was supposed to mean.

'I overheard my parents talking about me. I didn't like what
I heard. So I left.'

Her voice had been rough since it had come back. Throaty and
lower than usual—to Nick, it was incredibly sexy. With these
words, it broke. Zoe fumbled out another lozenge and put it in
her mouth, still manoeuvring the truck expertly through traffic.

He could imagine what she wasn't saying. How what she had

heard had hurt her; how much it still hurt her. He wanted to take her in his arms and hold the girl she had once been, the woman she had become.

'What made you go home?' he asked.

'Xenia. I went by her apartment every day, to see if she'd come back, and one day she had. She didn't ask any questions. She cleaned me up and took me out for a meal. I stayed with her overnight and then I went home. She didn't say anything. I just felt more like I could go home after I saw her.'

'I bet she knew,' Nick said.

'Now, I think she probably did.' Zoe pointed out the windshield again. 'A couple blocks down there is Radio City Music Hall and the Rockefeller Centre, and in a minute we're going to be driving into Times Square.'

Nick couldn't have cared less about the sights. All he was looking at was Zoe. 'What was living on the streets like?'

'It was scary. There were a lot of weirdos and perverts and a lot of people on drugs. But it was exhilarating at the same time, you know? There were no rules. I think I needed to prove to myself that I could do whatever I wanted.'

Nick nodded. 'I know what you mean about needing to prove things to yourself. You were right about my trying to prove I'm not like my dad. I do genuinely like animals and care about the environment. But I was trying to prove I was responsible.'

Zoe didn't answer for a few moments and, although Nick wanted to watch her, he looked out the window, finally seeing all the buildings and the lights and the cars and the people. There was something about her that made him feel she needed a little space, just for now.

'You were right, too,' she said quietly. 'I push people away. It's easier. Here's the Lincoln Tunnel under the Hudson.'

He kept on looking out the window, at the brick arches of the tunnel as they entered it, and then at the glossy tiled walls as they drove through it, the sound of traffic echoing in the enclosed space. For the moment, she'd stopped pushing him away. He could stop pushing, too.

It wasn't a mystery why he was so attracted to her, he thought. At first he'd compared her to his usual type of woman. He'd always liked delicate women, ones who were overtly feminine, ones who liked being protected and taken care of, having doors opened, being listened to, being helped. He liked taking care of them; he liked feeling strong and reliable.

And yet he had to admit that his past relationships had failed because being strong and reliable wasn't enough for him. After a while, he wanted more than being relied on. He wanted something back. Some excitement, some passion. Some of the same thing he felt when he was in the forest surrounded by plants eating sunlight and drinking rootwater, by animals busy living. He wanted that connection as deep as his soul.

And, yeah, he'd avoided relationships recently because he was scared, deep down, that he was like his dad, leaving when the going got too tough.

He glanced at Zoe. She was watching the traffic, both her hands on the wheel. The silver ring on her thumb gleamed in the sunlight. It was a reminder that she could take care of herself.

There was the answer to how he felt about her. He wasn't attracted to her despite her difference to his usual girlfriends; he was attracted to her because of her difference.

And he was so attracted to her that he was in danger of losing his mind to the influence of his gonads. In the small space of the cab, he breathed in her scent. They'd both changed out of their sweaty T-shirts but he could still smell the warmth of her skin. And she still wore her exercise shorts. His gaze dropped to the smooth skin of her thighs and he couldn't help imagining her wrapping her legs around his hips, clasping him closer, welcoming him inside her.

When he'd kissed her, she'd reacted with a passion he'd never experienced before. Her body wasn't only toned, it was responsive. And strong. Like the rest of her.

'So long Manhattan!' Zoe cried, and Nick looked up to see they were coming out of the tunnel. She was smiling again. Knowing her, she'd decided she'd had enough serious stuff for one day.

'You got any music in this wreck?' she asked, pulling a tape out of the deck and glancing at it. Her smile widened into a full-fledged grin. 'AC/DC? Ranger Giroux, you appear to rock!'

'It keeps me awake,' he said, and took the tape from her. He couldn't resist touching her fingers as he did. Then he put the tape into the player and turned the volume up, loud.

Zoe whooped as soon as the thumping bassline started. With quick jabs she rolled down the window and sang, her sore throat forgotten, her pensive mood gone, her past hurts and troubles put away as she told the New York they were leaving that she and Nick were on a highway to hell.

Nick laughed, and sang along with her.

'Roll down your window,' Nick said from the driver's seat.

Zoe opened her eyes. She hadn't quite drifted off, but the steady noise of the truck's engine and the darkness outside her window had lulled her into drowsiness. It was a long trip from New York to Maine, and they'd started pretty late in the afternoon. Nick had taken over driving somewhere in the morass of construction that was Connecticut and as they had made their way through Massachusetts and New Hampshire their conversation had faded to a comfortable silence. With her eyes closed, she'd let herself relax into the warmth of sitting next to Nick, and time had slipped away from her.

'Where are we?' she asked.

'Roll down your window and you'll find out.'

She couldn't see anything outside; the interstate was lit up, but their surroundings were black. The sky was much darker than it ever got in New York. She rolled down her window and Nick did the same.

'Now breathe,' he said.

She drew in a long, deep breath. The air was as cool as spring water. Carried on it was the scent and the taste of pine. Not like what counted for pine scent in air fresheners or cleaners; it was green and fresh and alive and it made her think of vast spaces, quiet woods, age and vitality.

Nick carried that scent with him.

'We're in Maine,' she said.

Nick let out his own breath and nodded. His face was lit up softly by the dash lights, emphasising his high cheekbones and straight nose, and the shadow of beard on his jaw. 'Not far from Kittery,' he said. He breathed in again. 'It's good to be home.'

Zoe sniffed in again and opened her mouth to say something smart about missing the traffic fumes, but there was a sudden bang and the truck jerked sharply to the left. She hung on hard to the armrest on the door as Nick wrestled the steering wheel, the truck swerving and squealing.

'Blow-out,' he muttered, and swore, but within seconds he'd gotten the truck under control and pulled it slowly onto the right shoulder.

'You okay?' he asked her immediately. Zoe unwrapped her hand from the armrest.

'Fine,' Zoe said. 'You?'

'Yeah.' He turned off the ignition.

'You think the bird's okay?'

'I'll check.'

Nick took a flashlight from the glove compartment and they both got out of the truck. Nick went to the back to check out the pigeon; Zoe went around the side to inspect the damage. The night air was cold and, glancing up, Zoe saw she'd been wrong. The sky wasn't darker than in New York. It was absolutely jam-packed with stars.

'Pigeon's fine,' Nick called.

'Your tyre isn't,' she replied. 'It's flatter than a pancake.'

Nick came round the side of truck and shone the flashlight down at the tyre. He swore again. She sort of liked the sound of him swearing. He swore like a guy who didn't swear that often but when he did, he meant it.

'It's no problem,' she said. 'We can change it in a jiffy. Where's your jack?'

'It's not as easy as that,' Nick said gloomily.

'What's the matter—don't you know how to change a tyre? Don't worry, I'm a pro. Get out the spare and I'll get started.'

'That is the spare,' Nick said.

Zoe put her hands on her hips. 'The spare? As in, the only spare?'

'Yup.'

'What happened to your "be prepared" motto, Boy Scout?'

'I punctured a tyre on a rock on a back road the morning before I went to Cranberry Island. I put the tyre in to be repaired and I was supposed to pick it up when I got back. But then when I got back, there was the letter from my dad, and I didn't want to wait so I just drove down on the spare.'

'That was stupid,' Zoe told him.

'I know.'

'I might've done the same thing, though.'

'That makes me feel better.' In the darkness she could just make out a wry smile.

'You got the number of a rescue service?'

'That, I am prepared for.' He pointed ahead of the truck. The headlights illuminated an emergency phone on a pillar a hundred yards or so ahead. 'Stay a safe distance from the truck. I'll be right back.'

Zoe watched him walking up the hard shoulder towards the phone. The headlights cast his shadow, long and broad shouldered, on the road ahead of him. They also illuminated his body perfectly. She could see the shape of the muscles of his shoulders and backside through the cotton of his T-shirt and shorts. Gorgeous man.

Strangely, she was glad he'd messed up by doing something so stupid as trying to drive nearly a thousand miles on his spare tyre. It meant he wasn't such a Boy Scout, such a white knight. He was just a guy who made mistakes.

She went to the back of the truck and, with a grunt, hauled out the animal carrier with the pigeon inside. There would be no point in having hauled the stupid bird several hundred miles if it was going to get killed by somebody driving into the back of the stationary truck. She climbed over the guard rail and up a bit of a grassy slope, set down the cage, and sat down next to it.

Her eyes had adjusted to the darkness and there was enough

light from the truck and the stars to see the pigeon through the slots in the plastic cage. It was a bird-shaped shadow, but she could catch a gleam of soft green from the feathers around its neck and she could see its face, lit up in a bar of light from the truck. It gazed back at her, its beady eye unabashed.

'Atta boy,' she murmured to it. 'You're not scared at all, are you?'

She shouldn't be scared, either.

She thought back to the conversation they'd had driving through New York. She'd never told anybody about that time she'd run away. Her parents had gone wild trying to find her, called the police and everything the day she'd left, but when she'd called from a pay phone in Grand Central Station the next morning they'd accepted her story that she was staying with Xenia. Xenia herself had never asked, even though she'd had to endure the lecture from Zoe's parents, too. Zoe had kept the whole thing a secret, her own private proof that whatever life threw at her, she would be okay. She could handle it.

But she'd told Nick. She'd opened herself up to him in a way she hadn't done with anybody for a long, long time. Because she trusted him, and she hadn't been afraid.

It felt really good.

Zoe lay back on the bank. The grass was cool and slightly damp, and felt soft on her bare legs and the back of her neck. She looked up at the millions of stars. She'd never seen so many all at once. It was as if she were on a whole new planet. The only reminder she was on Earth was the occasional noise of a car rushing past at sixty-five miles an hour.

She heard Nick walking back along the road and then she heard him approaching her on the grass. 'We're in luck,' he said. 'There's a rescue truck that's just finished a call close to here. They'll be here in ten minutes to tow us to a garage in Kittery.'

'That's good,' Zoe said dreamily. 'Come here and look at these stars.'

He lay down on the grass next to her, just a few inches away. She didn't take her eyes off the stars, but she could hear how close he was and feel the warmth of his body.

'I didn't think there were that many,' Zoe said.

'There's less light pollution here than in New York.' He settled himself comfortably, and she heard his soft breath of content-ment. This was where Nick belonged. 'And there's still quite a bit of light here in southern Maine. You should go to Baxter State Park, up in Piscataquis County. On a moonless night the stars are so bright you feel as if you could reach out and touch them.'

Zoe didn't think. She just did what she felt like doing without considering being afraid. She rolled over so that her body was lying on top of Nick's, and kissed him.

His lips were warm. He didn't seem surprised. He wrapped his arms around her, holding her close to his body, and kissed her back. Their mouths fitted together perfectly and so did their bodies and Zoe kissed him slowly and savoured every taste and texture of his mouth.

Desire flared in her, beading her nipples against his chest and sending a rush of warmth between her legs. She could feel his penis hardening underneath her. And yet she still kissed him slowly. She let her tongue touch his and let her lips sample his mouth. She wanted him. He wanted her. It was under control. She could handle it.

She separated their kiss into smaller, separate kisses, touching his top lip, his bottom lip, the corner of his mouth, dipping into his mouth, each one brief and tender. She could feel him smiling and she stopped, her face a fraction of an inch above his.

'This is very romantic,' he whispered to her.

She smiled back at him. 'Nobody's ever accused me of that bef—'

She was interrupted by the roar of an eighteen-wheeler thundering up the Turnpike past them.

Both of them laughed, and that thrust their bodies even closer together. The root of his erection rubbed hard between her legs, sending melting pleasure through her, and she gasped.

Nick stroked up her back and held her head in one large hand so his palm cradled the side of her face. 'I want you so much, Zoe,' he said. 'Don't push me away this time. Please.'

'You two need a tow or are you havin' too good a time?'

Zoe didn't get off Nick, but she did look over her shoulder. A tow truck had stopped on the shoulder behind Nick's truck, and a man in a plaid shirt and a baseball cap was leaning against it.

'Rescue's arrived,' she muttered, and rolled off Nick, but she made sure that as she did she pressed her breasts and hips as tightly against him as she could. Nick groaned quietly and she dropped another swift kiss onto his lips. 'Be patient,' she whispered, and then stood.

'We'll take a tow,' she said. 'Mr Bright Ideas here decided that driving round-trip to New York on his spare would be fun.'

'Ayuh, that was a bright idea, all right.' The man adjusted his baseball cap and then his jeans. 'Well, you climb into the cab and I'll hitch you up. I'll drop off your truck at Maddie's garage in Kittery, that's the closest place, but they won't be open at this hour. Won't get your tyre fixed till tomorrow mornin'.'

Nick had stood and joined her. He placed a warm hand on the small of her back, a possessive touch that made her shiver.

'Looks like we'll be staying in Kittery for the night,' he said. 'Is there a hotel you can drop us at?'

'Oh ayuh, there's plenty.'

'That's good. A hotel's much more comfortable than the side of the road,' he added in a low voice for Zoe's ears only, and gave her a long look that sent another shiver through her.

'Can't see the stars, though,' she replied. Her voice shook.

'It's not the stars I want to see.' He touched her lips, once, briefly with his finger, an invitation and a promise, and then he joined the man.

Zoe could join them. She knew everything about cars, she knew how to hitch up a car to be towed, and she could shoot the manly crap as well as either of them. She didn't have to wait in the cab of the truck like a helpless female.

But her blood was hot, her heart pounding, and every inch of her body was singing with anticipation and she wanted a moment to breathe. Because sex with Nicholas Giroux, if she had it, was going to be the experience of a lifetime and she wanted to calm down, slow down, get it right. Not rush in and fumble and mess it up.

She picked up the pigeon carrier, climbed into the tow truck, and rested it on her lap. *Breathe, Zoe,* she told herself. She took the pine- and motor-scented air deep into her lungs, in through her nose, out through her mouth, slowly and with discipline, as she'd trained herself to do as she exercised. And concentrated on her breathing, her body, her blood rushing through her veins. And nothing else.

Because if she really started thinking, she wouldn't touch Nicholas Giroux again.

CHAPTER ELEVEN

THE HOTEL WAS called The Lobster Trap. It didn't seem like an auspicious name, really.

Swinging the room key from her fingers, Zoe walked towards Nick where he stood in the motel parking lot, having just paid the tow truck driver. He had his backpack on his back, and Zoe's bag slung over one shoulder. When he saw her approach he bent to pick up the pigeon carrier case, too, but Zoe beat him to it.

'Where are we sleeping?' he asked cheerfully.

Zoe didn't think his choice of words was all that accurate. After their kiss, they'd spent half an hour together in the cramped space of the tow truck's cab. Her leg had pressed against his from hip to calf and even though he hadn't laid a hand on her she'd been aware of every breath he'd taken, every small movement of his body as the truck had juddered over the road.

He'd spent most of the journey chatting with the driver about the weather, the roads, the fact that they had a New York City pigeon as a passenger. Zoe had been able to get a couple of cracks in—that was until she'd let herself turn her face towards Nick and their eyes had met.

Even in the dark cab, she'd been able to see what he'd been thinking about. The fact that they were going to a hotel to make love with each other. And at the thought such a huge wave of desire had swept through her body that she hadn't trusted herself to speak again, for fear it would either come out as a squeak or a series of undignified horny gasps.

And now she was walking across the parking lot with him, towards the room where they would shortly engage in what she was sure would be the most pleasurable sexual intercourse she had ever experienced in her life.

'Room sixteen,' she said, checking the plastic fob on the room key and not meeting Nick's eyes. The motel was a motor court, with the rooms arranged in a low white clapboard building lining two sides of the parking lot. Zoe headed for the left hand side, without looking to see if Nick was following her; she knew he was. 'Right next to the ice machine, the lady said.'

'That'll be handy if we need cooling down,' Nick said. She didn't need to see his expression. The man was sex personified.

'You're a real smooth talker, do you know that?'

'Hey, you have to develop a good line in charm when you're trying to coax a wounded deer out of a thicket.'

'Well, I'm not a wounded deer.' She reached the door and slid the key into the lock. It took a little bit of jiggling before it turned.

'No, you certainly are not.' Nick stepped into the room after her and she barely had a chance to put down the pigeon and look around before his hands were on her shoulders, turning her gently around to face him.

'You're a sexy, intelligent, exciting woman,' he murmured. He trailed one of his fingertips down the side of her cheek and over her lips, so tender and warm it felt like a kiss. 'I'm glad you decided to get one room instead of two, Zoe.'

With his words she realised that he had arranged it on purpose so he had been busy paying the driver while she'd booked the room. He'd wanted to give her a choice about whether they'd share. About whether they'd sleep together.

'They weren't cheap,' she hedged, and then felt her cheeks flush as she realised what a stupid thing she'd said. 'Of course, I could probably buy the whole hotel if I wanted to, huh?'

'And the one next to it,' he agreed. 'We didn't even have to be in the same building if you didn't want to.'

'Well, we are,' she said, and turned away from him to look around the room. It was mainly decorated in the sort of orange that had been in style in the seventies. The carpet was burnt umber, the wallpaper was beige with terracotta diamonds, the bedside lamps were tangerine. There was a picture of a lobster on the wall.

And the bed was big. Big and bedlike and orange with some sort of wicker headboard. Big and obvious and unavoidable because that was the place where the two of them were going to have sex with each other, because Zoe had made that decision, she'd decided it as soon as she'd kissed Nick, she'd decided it when she'd decided to come with him to Maine, and she wanted to have sex with Nick more than she wanted anything else in the world so why was she getting cold feet now?

She turned back to Nick. He'd put down his pack and her bag and was standing watching her. He still wore his shorts, running shoes and T-shirt and the outfit left little to the imagination. She could see the strength of his shoulders, the broad outline of his chest. She remembered what he looked like without a shirt on, and what he'd felt like when she'd touched him in the gym. His legs were muscular, perfect. The man even had sexy knees. And at his crotch, the material of his shorts was beginning to tighten and outline his arousal.

Yeah. Sexy man. This was not the problem. She met his eyes and faced the problem.

His eyes were dark and intense. His mouth was both firm and gentle. His cheekbones were noble, his chin was masculine. He was absolutely everything she dreamed about in a man and she was right back to what she'd been afraid of in the gym because if she slept with him she was going to tumble right into stupid, idiotic, kick-yourself-in-the-head type love with him.

'Zoe?' he said softly, and didn't make a move towards her.

He was coaxing her. Like a damn injured deer.

Zoe straightened her spine at the realisation.

He thought she was afraid? He could have another think coming. She'd decided on a New York sidewalk to come up here to Maine with him and she'd decided by a Maine highway that she wasn't going to be scared of anything. And she wasn't.

This was Nick's world, pine scent and lobster and all. It wasn't her world. She wasn't staying here, and she could take care of herself, and when she went back to New York she could carry on from where she left off. Because she always had.

Zoe smiled at Nick. She'd show him how scared she was.

She grabbed the hem of her T-shirt and pulled it over her head.

Nick's eyes just about bugged out of their sockets. She saw him stare, saw him swallow, saw him not breathing. She watched his eyes travel over her chest. Her sports bra was black and not the most feminine thing on the planet, but Nick didn't seem to care.

Zoe knew she wasn't pretty, but she did like her body all right. She worked out just about every day; she was trim and fit and healthy and she'd had enough lovers to know that her body was attractive.

But the way Nick was staring at her was different from the way any other man had looked at her. He wasn't assessing her or ogling her.

He was looking at her as if she were a goddess.

'Zoe,' he said again, and this time it wasn't coaxing. It was raw and full of hunger.

He took a single step towards her and Zoe saw the outline of his erection, full length now and taut against his shorts.

She wasn't a goddess. But Nick wanted her, badly. And that made her feel powerful.

Zoe kicked off her sneakers and then hooked her fingers in the waistband of her shorts and pulled them down her legs. When she straightened up, she was wearing only her sports bra and her matching thong, and she could see Nick was breathing now, so hard he was nearly panting.

'I need a shower,' she said. 'How about you?'

And she turned and walked into the bathroom, not checking if he followed her.

The bathroom wasn't orange, mercifully, but it did have fish painted on the white tiles. The tub, with shower attached, wasn't that big—not really big enough to get up to what she wanted to get

up to in it. Zoe turned on the taps anyway and stood beside the tub
in her underwear, testing the water with her hand as it warmed.

She didn't hear him come in above the sound of the water but
she felt his hands, big and warm, settle around her waist, and she
felt his breath on the back of her neck. Zoe smiled and leaned
slightly back against Nick. He was still dressed and his T-shirt
felt soft against her bare skin, covering the hardness of his chest.

'What took you so long?' she murmured.

'I was trying to believe my luck.' He kissed her neck where
it joined her shoulders and she shivered. Then she felt him un-
fastening her bra and gently pushing it off her shoulders. Her
breasts were heavy and full, and her nipples puckered erect in
the now-steamy air.

Nick smoothed his hands down her naked back and then
stroked her underwear down over her hips and down her legs.
His soft hair feathered the skin of her bottom as he bent to pull
off the wisp of Lycra, and then his hands trailed up the backs of
her legs, over her buttocks and to her hips as he straightened.

She was naked in front of him. In his hands, open to his gaze
and his touch and his body.

She'd felt powerful. Now she felt like jelly.

Zoe turned around in his arms. The desire on his face nearly
took her breath away. *I wanted this guy from the minute I saw
him and now I'm going to have him,* she thought, and the thought
spread a smile all over her face.

'You're wearing too much,' she said, and tugged his T-shirt
up over his head. About time she got to do that after watching
him do it so many times and not being able to touch him. He
raised his arms obligingly to help her remove it and she was
treated to a close-up view of his naked chest, all his beautiful
bulging muscles and strong sinews and bones, the trail of dark
hair on his stomach.

'Wrestling with all that wildlife has been good to you,' she
said to him. Her voice was pretty shaky.

'Jumping up and down on that plastic thing has been good to
you,' he answered. His gaze was hot on her. 'You're gorgeous.'

She wanted to touch his skin. She didn't. Looking was enough pleasure for now; touching might be too much, too good. Instead she hooked her thumbs in the waistband of his shorts, her hands just brushing his firm belly, and pulled them down.

He helped her take those off, too. He had to, because when she saw his naked body she couldn't take her eyes off him long enough to push his shorts down his legs.

Nick naked was the most amazing sight she had ever seen in her life, ever.

He was tall and strong and every line of him was perfect, every muscle defined. He was even more desirable because she knew his muscles hadn't been built in the gym, in front of a mirror; they'd been built working, trying to make the world a better place.

His legs and chest were tanned and he had a band of paler skin where his shorts would cover him while he was working outside. The paler skin was still masculine, but something about it seemed more naked than the rest of him. His hip bones were visible under his skin and the line of dark hair on his stomach flared out at his crotch.

His penis was beautiful. Zoe wasn't the type to go around admiring male organs; they were there, they gave pleasure, sometimes they were pretty funny-looking. But Nick's was part of his strength and his desire. It was part of him. It jutted out from his body, heavy and hard and long, completely in proportion with the rest of his big, hard body, and every inch of it was perfect.

Slowly, she lifted her gaze from his crotch to his face. Nick was watching her as intently as she was watching him and they still weren't touching but meeting his eyes was a shock and a pleasure. As if he were inside her already.

The air was thick and charged and Zoe felt as if she were on the edge of an explosion.

'I have never wanted another woman as much as I want you,' Nick said to her. The words nearly made her groan.

'Nick, you're—'

You're too good for me. And I never want you to stop looking at me the way you are now.

'Get the soap,' she said, her voice husky, and stepped into the shower.

The hot, pounding water was no substitute for Nick's hot, pounding body, but it still felt good. Not a release, but a distraction, and her muscles were tight and sore from being in a car for hours and then holding herself tense next to Nick. She closed her eyes and let it roll over her skin and waited for Nick to join her.

The rattle of the shower curtain let her know he had stepped into the tub. She opened her eyes and the first thing she saw was his smile.

'Here you go,' he said. He had one of those little hotel soaps in his hands and he broke it in half and handed one half to her. The tub was too narrow for them both to stand underneath the spray; the water bouncing off Zoe's body hit his in small droplets. The steam had made his hair curl at the ends.

She ran the soap between her hands to work it up into a lather. 'Where do you want to get clean first, Boy Scout?'

'Everywhere,' he said.

He stood there, waiting for her to touch him. She rubbed her hands around the soap, up and down and around, feeling the friction, imagining what it would feel like to touch Nick. He would feel a million times better than this soap and her own palms.

What was she waiting for?

She knew why he was waiting. He was a damned gentleman, even stark naked in a shower.

And she was waiting, working this soap into a sliver, because…

'You're not scared, are you, Zoe?'

It was half in earnest, half a challenge. Zoe raised her chin and shook her wet hair back.

'It takes more than a naked man with a huge erection to scare me, Nick Giroux,' she said, dropping the soap, and put her hands on him.

His chest was warm and solid and slightly roughened by hair. Her fingertips, made slippery by the soap, slid on his skin, over his pecs and his collar-bone, up over his strong shoulders and back down. His nipples were hard and they rasped against her palms. His obliques, his abs, the shallow indent of his navel in his firm stomach. And then she curved her hands around to his backside and explored the perfect roundness of his glutes.

Nick groaned and he touched her.

She nearly purred as his hands, slick with soap, started at her waist and skimmed up, leaving a trail of lather, over her ribs and to her breasts. And then all her hesitation was gone, down the drain like the water in the shower and she pulled him towards her with her fingertips digging into his buttocks and he met her halfway and kissed her.

His erection poked hard against her belly, and her breasts slipped over the skin of his chest, and their kiss was instantly carnal and desperate and far, far hotter than the shower. Zoe arched up into Nick and kissed him with all the pent-up desire she'd had building inside her since the first moment she'd seen him waiting outside her great-aunt's front door. He groaned again, deep in his throat. Zoe could feel the vibration of his voice in his lips, and it made her kiss him harder, wilder.

Nick. The perfect man, hers for this moment. When they broke for breath he smiled at her.

'You don't hold back when you go for it, do you?' he said.

'No, I don't.' She pulled him even closer and kissed him some more.

Nick manoeuvred them so that she was pressed back against the wall of the shower, pinned between the wet tiles and his hot wet body. Zoe lifted her knee and wrapped it around his hip. The position meant that the underside of his erection was in direct contact with her clitoris and the pleasure was so great she gasped into his mouth.

Since she'd lost her virginity at sixteen, just to get it out of the way, she hadn't slept around, but she'd had her share of lovers. None of them had ever made her feel like this: powerful and powerless, and desperate with a need so big that she didn't know if it could ever be fulfilled.

She tilted her hips so that she slid upwards along his slick length. Nick broke their kiss and, with one hand on her face, looked directly into her eyes. 'Tell me what you feel,' he said.

She moved again, sliding back down on him, and Nick made that guttural sound in his throat. His eyes were dilated, making them even darker than usual, and she knew that in one way she and he were feeling exactly the same thing. The same pleasure, the same desire, the same passion as the hot water pounded down on both of them.

And she felt more than that.

Zoe rubbed against him, building the friction, so wonderful it was almost maddening, and Nick matched her rhythm with his hips. The strokes were long and thrilling and Nick was clenching his teeth, his brows drawn together, his face a picture of a man trying to keep his ecstasy under control. Trying to make it good for her. Like a white knight.

'What do you feel?' he gritted.

She stared into his face, his strength and kindness. She knew what it was like to fight for control. Unlike him, it wasn't her body she had to worry about. She could let her body feel every sensation, grab every bit of bliss.

'I feel like I'm about to come,' she said to him, and that wrenched another groan from him. He tightened his hands on her and quickened his movements.

Two more strokes, three, and she gasped as the feeling heightened and then broke through her in waves. She dug her fingers into his flesh and held on to him, the one steady thing in a world that was splashing, dissolving.

She threw her head back against the shower wall, squeezed her eyes tight shut, and groaned out her climax. When she opened her eyes again Nick was looking straight down into them. He'd stopped moving, his erection still pressed tight against her and harder than ever.

'Wow,' he said.

'Tell me about it,' she breathed, and brought her mouth up to kiss him as wildly and passionately as she knew how. She'd just come and she wanted more. She wanted all of him.

'I need you inside me,' she panted when they broke apart.

'I think I need it worse,' Nick said, 'but we need protection, too.'

That brought her back down to earth with a thump. 'Damn. I haven't got—'

'I've got some in my backpack.' He gave her a crooked, sexy grin. 'Be prepared.'

'I've never been so thankful for the Boy Scout motto in my life,' said Zoe. She unwrapped her leg from around him. For a fleeting moment she thought about how she'd taken her pleasure and shown him how much she loved it. How she'd been wide open and honest, so honest that it made her a little afraid.

And then she looked at Nick again, his face wet and flushed with desire, his chest heaving with his quick breaths, his penis hard up against his body. No way was she going to be scared now.

She reached down and wrapped her hand around his erection, loving it how he sucked in his breath sharply at her touch. 'Let's go get these condoms,' she said, and turned her body and stepped backwards out of the tub, keeping her grip on his penis, leading him with her.

They didn't bother with towels but walked, dripping wet, straight into the bedroom and to his backpack. Zoe didn't take her hand off Nick as he unzipped a side pocket and got out a box of condoms. She noticed his hands were shaking.

'Now,' she said, and turned him around with her other hand, backed him towards the bed, and pushed him down on it, tumbling on top of him.

Their wet skin was slick against each other and though Zoe was impatient to have Nick inside her she kissed him again and he ran his hands all over her, their bodies so hot she could have sworn they were making steam.

And then she could not wait any longer. She reached for the box of condoms Nick was holding and he gave it to her.

'You're in charge,' he said.

Zoe knew he was talking about more than the condom.

She smiled, took the box, and sat upright, straddling his naked body. With impatient fingers she pulled out a condom and tore open its wrapper. Then both her hands were on him again, rolling the condom down over his rigid length.

She should savour the feeling, she should experience every inch of him in case she only got to do this once, but she couldn't go slow. She wanted to get this condom on him as quickly as she could because as she put it on him she heard him groan and she wanted to hear the noise he made when he was inside her. When he was coming.

Zoe raised herself on her knees and positioned herself above him, her fingers still wrapped around his penis. Nick grasped her hips with his hands but he didn't guide her. Just held her. Because she was in charge.

'I'm going to give you the ride of your life,' she said, and sank down onto him.

She was so turned on, so wet and ready that he slid in quickly, big as he was, all the way up to the hilt, and Zoe gasped and heard Nick groan again.

'Zoe, you're incredible,' he said.

He was incredible. He stretched her, filled her, felt exactly right and she rotated her hips just to understand even more how great this was and then Nick's hands were on her breasts, and she lost control.

With a ragged cry she moved on him. She reared herself up, plunged back down, thrust her body against him and him into her as hard as she could. Below her Nick moved with her, his face tightened with pleasure, all his restraint gone. She could see his muscles tensing as he thrust into her, as she thrust onto him.

Wilder and faster, faster and wilder. Zoe felt the sweat break out on her body and she cried out, pulsing and squeezing around Nick as she came.

And then Nick roared out his own climax and she collapsed on his chest. Both of them breathing hard, bodies wet, hearts hammering in time.

He held her. He pushed back her damp hair and kissed her. He whispered, 'Zoe.'

She sighed in contentment and Nick pulled the blankets up over them. He curled her into his body, his arms tight around her, and they let their breathing slow and settle into sleep.

Zoe had never felt so safe.

CHAPTER TWELVE

HE WAS GONE.

Zoe woke up all at once and sat up in bed, her chest clogged with panic. The pillow beside her still held the indentation of Nick's head and there was a faint warm patch where he had lain. But he wasn't there, wasn't holding her and he had probably seen sense and booked it out of there as fast as he could go.

A scrap of paper on the orange bedspread caught her eye and she grabbed it. 'Gone to get the truck and breakfast, be back in a few,' it said. She hadn't seen Nick's handwriting before but she recognised him in its economical strokes. It was the way he moved.

She settled back into the warmth he'd left behind, and thought about the way Nick moved. The way he'd moved in the dark of last night, for example, when he'd woken her to have sex again. It had begun slowly, with soft kisses, but then hunger had taken over. Her otherwise-trained thigh muscles felt stiff, because she hadn't quite practised the exercise of wrapping her legs around a man's back and urging him to go faster, harder, deeper.

A smile touched her lips. She raised his pillow to her face and inhaled his scent left behind on the fabric. It was warm and arousing. If she'd woken up first, there was no way she'd have had the strength to get up and leave him there in bed without putting her hands all over him again.

Her smile faded. She wouldn't have been able to leave. But he had.

She swung her legs out of bed. God, what was the matter with her? She'd spent the night having the best sex in her entire life and she was getting all neurotic because she hadn't gotten laid yet today? Just because she was some sort of horn dog didn't mean that the man shouldn't go get his truck.

And it wasn't as if he would have suddenly seen her by the light of day and thought she was ugly. He'd seen her plenty in the light of day before. It wasn't as if sex with her would have cleared his vision or anything, like kissing a frog in reverse.

A noise from the corner caught her attention. The pigeon was cooing and shifting around in its cage, which was still sitting on the desk near the door, where she'd put it down last night. Zoe stood, pulled on a T-shirt and a pair of jeans from her bag, and went over to the cage. There was an open bag of birdseed next to it; Nick must have fed the pigeon its breakfast before he went out to find theirs.

Zoe sat down in the chair next to the desk and opened the plastic door of the cage. The pigeon didn't start or back away. It cocked one bright beady eye at her.

In the morning sunlight, the pigeon's feathers were a deep, soft grey, barred with black on the wings. Its neck gleamed green and blue, the colour of motor oil in water, but alive. Its eyes weren't black, as she'd thought, but orange around a dark pupil.

There was food in its dish, but Zoe put a few more seeds in. Then she carefully pushed the dish closer to the bird.

'Come on and get it, the room service isn't going to last for ever,' she whispered to it.

It watched her for a few seconds, and then dipped its head and snapped up a seed with its black beak. Its neck feathers rippled and glowed as it swallowed and pecked for another seed. Every move was sure and almost defiant of her, as if the pigeon knew Zoe was there, all right, but decided it couldn't be bothered to care about her presence.

'You're one tough fella,' she said. The bird's rounded head and glowing neck swelled out to a plump, graceful breast and body. She remembered New York pigeons in flight, clapping their wings and soaring above the traffic and noise. A connection between the ground and the sky. She wondered if its feathers would be soft. They looked soft.

'Nobody thinks you're very special, huh?' she said. 'They think you birds are all alike and you're all pests. But you don't care.'

The pigeon made a sound in the back of its throat.

'The thing is, I care what Nick thinks. I really care. That's not good.' She sighed. 'I even liked sleeping with him holding me. Usually, I hate sharing my space.'

She picked up one of the seeds and bit it. It didn't taste like much. No wonder pigeons liked picking through the garbage. She'd rather have an old hot dog bun herself.

She was absent-mindedly raising another seed to her mouth when the lock rattled and Nick walked into the room.

'Boy you must be really desperate for breakfast,' he said.

This morning he looked even more gorgeous than he ever had before. Maybe it was because she'd slept with him, and seen and touched every part of his body. Maybe it was the extra-sexy glint in his eyes as he looked at her.

She closed the pigeon's cage and stood up. 'That's not all I'm desperate for,' she said.

Nick dropped a paper bag on the desk, came over to her, and took her in his arms. He was cold from the morning air. It felt wonderful.

'I'm so relieved to see you,' Nick murmured, stroking her hair with one hand and letting the other trail over her back and buttocks.

'Where was I going to go?' She kissed him on the side of his jaw. He hadn't shaved for two days, according to her count, and the stubble was beginning to get soft. 'And how? You were getting the truck.'

'Knowing you, you'd go anywhere and any way you could.' He kissed her forehead, her eyebrows, the tip of her nose. 'I broke the speed limit all the way back here from the garage because I was sure you were going to be gone when I got back.'

So the whole time she was worried about why he was gone,

he was worrying about her leaving? Zoe shook her head and un-buttoned his shirt to feel his bare skin.

'I'm not going anywhere,' she said. 'After all this, I have to see your father with my own eyes. Besides, you wouldn't be able to get into Xenia's house without me.'

Zoe finished unbuttoning his shirt and let out a low moan of delight at the feeling of his naked chest under her hands. There was a special bliss at being skin-to-skin with Nick.

'I hope you stayed for me, as well as my dad,' he said to her.

'Well, you have your uses.' She kissed his collar-bone and let the sparse hair on his chest tickle her nose. His nipple, erect and dark brown, looked so tempting she licked it, and she felt him shudder.

He took her head in his hands and lifted her face so she was looking at him. 'I'm glad you're here. I haven't been able to think about anything except for last night, you and me together. I knew it was going to be good, Zoe, but not that good.' He dropped a kiss on her lips. 'You completely blew my mind.'

Likewise. 'Being on that island really made you desperate, huh?'

He shook his head. 'It's you, Zoe. I've never been to bed with a woman like you.'

And was this a good thing? Or was this just a little excursion into unknown territory, a little walk on the wild side, before Nick went back to his normal life and his normal women?

And why should she be worried about that, since she was planning on going back to her normal life herself?

'And what kind of woman am I?'

He slid his hand down from her face, over her neck and curled it around her breast. Zoe inhaled sharply and arched up into him. His erection, through his jeans, pressed against her stomach.

'Someone who takes charge,' he said. 'Who knows what she wants and goes for it.'

'I know what I want right now.' She slid her hands between them and tugged open his jeans. The fingers of both her hands wrapped around his penis, rock-hard and hot. He jerked against her, into her hands. The memory of him inside her made her groan at the same time that he did.

The future didn't matter; what mattered was right here and now, Nick with her, his sex in her hands, their bodies burning. He liked her being strong. And she felt strong and free and wonderful.

And this was good. This was better than good. Being with Nick, even though it made all of her doubts and fears crowd into her head, even though it made her more desperate and wanting than she'd ever been before, made her feel the best she had ever felt.

She smiled and slowly sank down, letting her body rub against his, until she was on her knees in front of him. He still wore his jeans and his boxers, but his penis in her hands protruded from his open fly, at the level of her face.

She loved the sight of his erection, hard and long and deep red at its sculpted tip. She could feel the heat from him on her face.

Zoe licked her lips, and she heard him hitch in a breath and saw his penis jerk in anticipation. Then she couldn't hold back any longer; she touched him with her lips and tasted him with her tongue. The textures were incredible, smooth skin stretched taut over hardness that throbbed with his heartbeat. She held him with both hands and sucked him deep into her mouth, swirling her tongue over the tip.

'Zoe,' Nick groaned, and his voice made her hungrier, made her take him deeper, caress him more quickly.

He reached down and lifted her to her feet. 'I need to be inside you,' he said to her and swept her up into his arms and carried her over to the bed.

When had a man picked her up before? As if she were a delicate fairy princess or something? It didn't even seem like an effort to Nick.

He laid her on the bed and she pulled him down with her. He landed on top of her and she laughed, loving his weight pressing her into the bed.

The laughter became a gasp as his mouth came down on hers, strong and possessive. He yanked her T-shirt up over her breasts and lowered his head to suck at her nipple, as hungrily as she'd sucked at him.

Without looking, her eyes locked on Nick's head at her breast,

Zoe reached over and grabbed a condom from the bedside table. Nick took it from her and within seconds he had it on and had tugged her jeans down her legs and was positioning himself between her legs. Zoe twined her legs with his, the denim of his jeans rough on her bare thigh. She pulled him closer, dying to feel him thrusting inside her.

But he paused, every muscle tense, holding himself above her with his arms. His shirt was open, his jeans pushed down, and she still wore her T-shirt rucked up over her screamingly sensitive breasts.

'Nick,' she said, knowing she was begging, and for once not caring.

'I've never met anyone like you,' he said. 'Someone who acts equal to me, who's just as strong. You're incredible, Zoe.'

The tip of his penis was just at the entrance to her body. One movement, one fraction of an inch, and he would be inside her again. Zoe arched against him, squirmed, tried to push herself closer, to be joined with this man, to lose herself in the wild pleasure of his lovemaking, and stop thinking about what he was saying. Because he was nearly right. They were equal: in passion, in abilities, in fitness, in pride.

They were equal in just about every single way except for one. Because she loved him.

Then Nick shifted his body on hers. He entered her, filled her, gave her nearly everything she wanted, and Zoe gasped and stopped thinking.

Nick smiled as Zoe reached over and stroked his jaw and chin one more time. Even such a simple touch was exciting. He glanced away from Route 3 to smile at her.

'You'd think I'd never shaved before,' he said.

'You've never had a clean-shaven face when I could touch you,' she answered promptly, and stroked her fingers over his chin again. 'I like you all fresh and smooth.'

'I thought you liked the rugged, manly Mountain Man stuff.'

'Oh, I do.' Her voice went lower, and Nick glanced away

from the road again to see her wide, sexy smile. 'I like it very much. I've got stubble marks all over my body to prove how much I like it.' She pulled out the neck of her T-shirt and showed him a red mark on her fair skin, where he'd kissed and nipped at her collar-bone this morning, on his way downwards to her gorgeous breasts.

He had to force himself to look back at the road before he drove into the back of the pulp truck ahead of him.

He wanted her even more than he had before. It was as if making love to her only confirmed and added to his attraction, made him learn more about why she was desirable.

This was definitely something that had never happened to him before.

He took his right hand off the wheel and ran it slowly up the firm length of her thigh. He heard Zoe sigh in pleasure at the caress. This was another thing. Her body was beautiful, even sexier than he'd imagined after seeing her in skimpy Lycra. But it wasn't just her body that drove him wild. It was her, her softness inside, her unashamed passion. The way she was putty in his hands one moment and the next moment was taking charge. A confident, smart-mouthed woman; an uncertain, vulnerable woman; a sexy, feminine, strong woman; a bundle of contradictions that added up to the most fascinating person he'd ever met.

'How much longer till Southwest Harbour?' Zoe asked.

'With off-season traffic, it'll take us about fifteen minutes from the bridge onto Mount Desert Island. Which is just up there.' He pointed.

Zoe rolled down the window to look, and then she withdrew her head quickly. 'Ugh. I thought you said Maine smelled good.'

'That's the salt marshes. It smells better on the island.' Nick squeezed her thigh and thought about her smell. Soap, skin, that elusive perfume, Zoe warmth. The places where her smell was most her: between her breasts, on the inside of her thigh, on the side of her neck. He felt his loins stirring.

'Where do you live?'

'I've got a cabin on the mainland, on a lake not far from

Ellsworth that we just drove through. Property on the island is expensive.'

'You live back there? Why didn't we stop? You must be sick of living out of a backpack.'

'I'm used to it.' He glanced over at her again. 'You're right, though. We should have stopped. I haven't had sex with you for about four hours, and I've got a double bed at home.'

Zoe grinned. 'I'm sure my great-aunt's house has plenty of beds. And couches. And tables. And—'

'Stop talking about it or I'm going to drive us off the road,' Nick groaned. The stirring in his pants had grown to epic proportions.

Uncomfortable as his raging erection made him, he couldn't help but appreciate the difference between this drive up to Maine with Zoe, and his drive alone down to New York. On his way to New York, he'd driven fast, had only stopped when absolutely necessary, his brain spinning on the letter his father had written, his veins thrumming with rage.

On this drive, his brain was spinning on Zoe, his veins thrumming with desire. He could honestly say he hadn't thought about his father more than once or twice.

And that was pretty unexpected, too.

Zoe laughed. 'What do you want to talk about?'

'Something completely non-sexual, please.'

'How about the pigeon? He's getting better, isn't he? What are you going to do with him?'

'Her.'

'What?'

'The pigeon's a female.'

'How can you tell?'

Nick shrugged. 'Practice. She's smaller than a male.'

'Huh.' Zoe seemed to think about that for a minute. 'Anyway, what are you going to do with her when she's all better? Let her go up here in Maine?'

'That's the plan. She'll be able to join a flock up here. Hopefully she won't miss the New York smell and traffic too much.'

'She might. Not all of us hate it as much as you do, remember.'

Nick turned off Route 3 towards Southwest Harbour. With the pulp truck not in front of him any more, he could drive faster, the sooner to get to their destination and get his hands all over Zoe.

'I could always bring her back to New York with me when I go,' Zoe said.

Nothing changed. The road was still clear in front of him, the truck was still rolling forward, the sun was still shining, and Nick's world flipped over and fishtailed out of the direction he'd been happily following for the past twenty-four hours.

Nick kept his hands on the wheel, his foot on the gas, and kept driving.

She was leaving him.

'That's an idea,' he said, lightly, feeling his hands clench on the wheel so hard his knuckles hurt. 'Tell me something, Zoe. Since when are you so fond of the vermin?'

'She's sort of grown on me.' Her cheerful voice showed no awareness of how Nick was feeling.

Of course not. She'd never planned on staying with him. First, she'd done her utmost to try to force him away. And then she'd come along with him on a temporary trip. As a temporary lover. Which was just exactly the same way she'd accused him of trying to treat her.

'When are you thinking of going back to New York?' he asked, gritting his teeth.

He didn't look, but he could feel her shrug. 'Well, sooner or later I've got to face up to this inheritance and decide what I'm going to do about it. I've decided that annoying my family isn't really good enough motivation; I'm going to have to do something useful with it. But before that I've got to see what your dad looks like. The curiosity is killing me.'

'Let's find my dad, then.'

They'd reached the town of Southwest Harbour, and were driving down the main road, lined with pastel-painted wooden businesses. Nick braked, pulled the truck over into a parking space with a jerk of the steering wheel, and threw it into neutral. Without looking at Zoe he opened the door and got out.

She caught up with him halfway to the general store. 'You all right, Nick?'

No. And of course, he was still turned on. Apparently he had no trouble lusting after Zoe while he was angry at her. Hopefully the inhabitants of Southwest Harbour wouldn't notice the flagpole in his jeans.

'I want to ask if anybody here knows my father before we go storming up to Xenia's house.' He pushed open the store door and walked in amidst the jangling of the bell. He knew Zoe was behind him because he knew every single breath she took and had for the past few days.

Not that it was going to make much difference.

The general store was set up for tourists and summer people; the refrigerator was full of imported beer and the shelves were full of expensive groceries. Nick picked up a *Bangor Daily News* and put it on the counter, staffed by a middle-aged man in a flannel shirt.

'Afternoon,' he said, letting his voice relax into Downeast vowels. 'Nice day.'

'Yup, good day for it.' The shopkeeper took his money and handed over change. 'You folks here for long?'

'That depends. Do you know a man called Eric Giroux? I think he might live around here, or be visiting.'

The man's face contracted in thought. 'I don't know an Eric, but there's Duck, up off Seal Cove Road. I think his last name is something like Giroux. One of those French ones, anyway.'

Duck. Nick remembered an orange hunting jacket, a whistle that made duck calls. 'That could be Eric,' he said.

'Keeps to himself, mostly. He's caretaker to a couple of the big houses that belong to summer people. It's a dirt road turnoff on the left, got a snowmobile trail sign marking it, if it's where I'm thinking.'

Zoe had been standing beside him, though he'd kept his eyes carefully off her. Now she said, 'We're also looking for Xenia Drake's house. I've got the address, but it's pretty vague.'

The man smiled. 'Oh, ayuh, Xenia. She's up off the Seal

Cove Road, too. I think Duck takes care of her place. Usually she comes by on her way up there. I haven't seen her for a few weeks, though.'

'She died,' Zoe said quietly, and although Nick was still angry he was also proud of the calm dignity in her voice. 'I'm her great-niece, Zoe Drake.' She held out her hand, and the man shook it.

'Oh. I'm real sorry to hear about that. Real sorry. Xenia was a character. We'll miss her around here.'

'Yes, I'll miss her, too.'

Nick didn't feel like hearing about people missing other people they'd lost. He thanked the shopkeeper and went outside, back to the truck.

Zoe joined him a few moments later. She had a paper bag full of groceries. 'That's great news, huh? He's here. Looks like you didn't have any reason to go all the way to New York after all.'

No reason, in the end, except to meet a woman who was different from anybody he'd ever met before, both in bed and out of it.

'Well, at least I rescued the pigeon,' he said, and climbed into the truck. 'Let's go.' He started the engine while she walked around the truck, and pulled away from the parking spot while she was still buckling her seat belt.

'Geez, I thought you animal-rescue type people had to be patient,' she commented.

'Zoe, I think it's reasonable that now that I'm about to see my father, I'm feeling a little impatient.'

'Sure,' she said, her voice quiet again, and Nick realised he'd spoken both loudly and abruptly.

He also realised he'd told a lie.

Because he wasn't impatient to see his father. Aside from the automatic process of asking the shopkeeper questions, he hadn't been thinking about his father at all.

All he'd been thinking about was Zoe. Who was sitting right beside him, being supportive, and who hadn't left yet.

It was his father he should be angry about. He'd known Zoe for less than a week, and they'd made no commitment to each other. His father, on the other hand, had married his mother and produced two children before he'd walked out for ever.

He thought about his father as he turned the truck around and drove to Seal Cove Road. He knew the road; it crossed Acadia National Park, where he'd been working for the past four years. He'd driven on it and walked on it hundreds of times.

And so had his father. There might have been times when they were both on the same road at the same time. They might have passed each other without Nick even knowing.

'You okay, Boy Scout?'

He was sitting forward in his seat, every muscle tensed, his foot heavy on the accelerator. Zoe touched him lightly, on the back of the neck. He drew in a breath and did his best to relax, though it didn't work so well.

'I'm just wondering how long he's lived so close to me, and whether he knew I worked here all the time.'

'Looks like you'll find out soon,' Zoe said, and pointed to the dirt road turnoff on their left, marked by an orange snowmobile sign. Nick slowed the truck and pulled into the road.

It was full of potholes and wound uphill through the woods. Every jolt of the truck made Nick's muscles tense more, as if he were weathering a battery of light punches leading up to a final assault.

He'd thought about this moment for sixteen years. Ever since he'd turned off his cartoons and joined his mother at the telephone to hear that his father was gone.

Zoe's hand, still on the back of his neck, tightened and he saw that the dirt road ended at a battered white mobile home. There was a wooden shed built next to it, nearly half the size of the mobile home and in much better shape.

He keeps his tools in there, Nick thought. He turned off the truck and stepped out, in front of his father's house.

He knew Eric Giroux lived here. It wasn't the instant emotional connection he'd been half expecting; the place didn't look familiar at all, and he didn't have any sort of a feeling about it. Instead, it just made sense. He could imagine his father living in a place like this, in the middle of the woods, with a big new shed for his tools and hunting equipment—much more than he could imagine his father living in New York.

Nick heard Zoe getting out of the truck behind him. Her feet crunched on the dirt road. The only other noise was from the woods: the wind in the trees, a woodpecker, a chickadee. This was what his father would hear all day. The same thing Nick did.

The trailer was propped up on concrete blocks. Nick climbed the wooden stairs to the door and knocked. The sound vibrated through the whole trailer.

'Dad?' Nick called. 'It's Nick.' His voice sounded both loud and smaller, as if he were suddenly younger.

'I don't think he's here, Nick,' Zoe said behind him.

'Dad?' Nick knocked again, hearing this time that there was no noise from inside the trailer at all. All the windows were shut. He turned and scanned the site. For the first time he noticed his truck was the only vehicle parked on the drive.

He tracked animals as part of his job, made observations about habitats, and he hadn't noticed that basic fact? He shook his head to clear it and had a good look around.

His father wasn't there, all right. But the place wasn't abandoned; there were fairly recent tyre tracks on the dirt road, and he could see boot marks besides his own on the path leading to the trailer. The padlock on the shed door was both big and fairly new. The grass around the trailer had been cut in the past week or so. He hadn't noticed a mailbox, so his father probably picked up his mail in town.

There was nothing obvious like a delivered newspaper to show him how long his father had been gone, and he wasn't sure what the weather had been like here, but from instinct he felt his father had left probably anywhere from half an hour to twenty-four hours ago, but not much more than that.

Nick tried the door of the trailer. It was locked. In the woods of Maine, with a house owned by a Mainer, that probably meant the owner had gone away for more than a couple of hours.

Nick sat down on the wooden stairs and propped his chin in his hands.

Zoe approached him. 'Are you okay?'

'Fine. Looks like I'll be camping outside *this* door for a while now.'

He felt disappointment in his throat and swallowed it. He'd waited this long, he could wait a little longer.

The muffled sound of a phone ringing disturbed the sounds of the woods. Nick recognised it right away as his own cell phone. Reception wasn't always great on Mount Desert Island, but they must be close enough to Southwest Harbour to get a signal. He got up, went to the truck, and got the phone out of his glove compartment. The number on the screen was his sister Kitty's.

'Kit, you will never believe where I am,' he said into the phone.

'You'll never believe who I just saw.'

Nick leaned back against the truck. He had an idea what his sister was going to say, but she sounded too normal and cheerful for that to be true.

'Who?'

'Dad. He showed up around lunchtime, out of the blue.'

'Dad showed up at your house?' He stood up straight. Zoe was watching him from near the trailer, her hands on her hips.

'No, at my office. He said he got the address out of the yellow pages. We went back to the house for lunch.'

'You had lunch with our father?' His voice was loud and incredulous. Zoe started walking toward him.

'Yeah, well, it was lunchtime, and I thought he should meet Jack.'

Nick tried to picture his sister, his brother-in-law, and his father all sitting around Kitty's beautifully designed kitchen table eating tuna sandwiches. He couldn't do it.

'Does Mom know?'

'Yeah, she called while he was there and I told her. You know Mom. She didn't even act surprised.'

That, he could picture. Their mother took everything in her stride.

'What did you talk about?' he asked.

'Just—catching up, you know. He said he went to your

house this morning, but you weren't in, so he decided to drive down to Portland to see us instead. Where are you—in New York still?'

'No, I'm standing outside of Dad's house in Southwest Harbour.'

Kitty laughed. 'That's pretty funny.'

Nick didn't see the funny side at all. 'He's been living in Maine all this time.'

'Not all this time, apparently, but for the past few years, I guess. He's had jobs here and there. Now he takes care of some people's summer homes.'

'I know.'

'Yeah? How did you find all that out? He said he hadn't seen you yet. I told him you were in New York looking for him, and he couldn't figure out why you would go there. He's never been there, he said. How'd you trace him back to Maine?'

'It's a long story.' Nick glanced at Zoe, who was watching him closely. 'What did he say?'

'I told you. He's lived all kinds of places, but now he's in Maine, and he decided it was time to see us, I guess.'

'I mean, what did he say about why he left?'

There was a pause on the other end of the line. Nick held his breath.

'We didn't talk about that.'

His breath whooshed out in incredulity and frustration. 'What? You mean he didn't apologise for leaving? He didn't even *explain* it to you?'

By now Zoe was standing right next to him. Knowing her, she was trying to say something, but he couldn't hear much but his sister's voice and his own heart pounding in his ears.

'No. It was—it was all right, Nick.'

'All right?'

He heard Kitty let out a gentle sigh. 'Listen. He said he was going to stay the night in Portland at a hotel, and head up north tomorrow. He'll probably be there by noon. You can talk to him then, if you want.'

'Oh, I want to.'

'And then let's talk, Nick. I'll come up there this weekend, okay? I'm worried about you.'

She'd just had lunch with their father and not even asked about why he'd betrayed her and the rest of the family—and she was worried about *him?*

'Sure. I'll see you tomorrow or Sunday.' He hung up the phone, and then punched the side of his truck hard enough to make a dent. 'Damn!'

'Hey.' He felt Zoe's hand on his arm. 'That truck is ugly enough without you making it worse.'

'He went to see my sister,' Nick told her. 'And he didn't even have the decency to say he was sorry for walking out on us. He just waltzed in there and had lunch with her like he was some kind of real father.' He kicked the nearest truck tyre.

'Well, he is your real father, Nick.'

Nick stopped and looked at her. 'What?'

She put both her hands on her hips again and faced him straight on, her jaw set, her eyes sparking. 'I don't usually give advice to people, so you should listen up good, Boy Scout. Back in New York, you said that my family try to reach out to me and all I do is push and push them away. Well, your father might have left you, but he wrote you a letter and now he's gone to find your sister. If that's not some kind of an apology, I don't know what is.'

'It's too late.'

'It might be, but that's not for you to decide until you've heard what he has to say. If you're not going to let me get away with rejecting my family, I'll be damned if I'm going to let you get away with rejecting yours.'

He looked at Zoe. Bold, strong, and throwing his own words back in his face. He had the distinct impression that if he didn't listen to her, she'd offer to kick his ass.

He felt a smile growing inside him, just a little one, but big enough to relax his shoulders, free his breathing.

'Since when did you get all compassionate and understanding?' he asked her.

She shrugged. 'It must be the pollution-free air.'

His smile reached the surface, and he saw her smile back.

'Is he going to be back here soon?' she asked.

'Not till tomorrow, probably.'

'Then let's go find Xenia's and get changed and go for a run or something. We've both been cooped up too long.' She stepped closer, stroked back his hair, and kissed him on the cheek.

Zoe had kissed him in passion. But this, Nick realised, was the first of a different kind of kiss from her: tender, caring, protective.

He took her hand and squeezed it. 'You're right. Let's go and enjoy the rest of the day.' He watched her climb back into the truck, and wondered if the rest of the day was all he was going to have with her.

CHAPTER THIRTEEN

As soon as they broke through the trees and Zoe saw the house she knew that she was home.

It was set back on a small rise, on a lawn surrounded by trees. The house was steep-roofed, generous in size, with brown-painted clapboards and tall windows framed by green shutters. A pot of geraniums sat on the porch next to a pair of rocking chairs. There was a bench underneath a tall pine tree on the front lawn and a picnic table in the sun.

Nick turned off the truck and for a moment she didn't move. She listened to the engine ticking and looked at the house. Then she threw open the door and ran up the lawn and up the three broad steps to the porch.

There was a screen door and then a thick wooden door and the keys the lawyer had given her fitted easily. She stepped into the cool house. It was all one room downstairs, living room and dining room and kitchen all together, bright with the afternoon sun.

Zoe stopped. 'Nick,' she said.

'Nice place.' He was right behind her, then beside her.

'This is where she wrote,' she said. She pointed to a vast wooden desk, facing out the back window of the house with a view of green-lit trees. A desktop computer sat next to stacks of paper. Beside the desk, a tall bookcase held Xander Dark hardbacks.

'It's different from her apartment,' Nick observed. He touched a chair back with one hand by way of illustration. It was simple, wooden, with a woven seat and a patchwork cushion. Like all the other furniture in the room it was functional, plain, and comfortable. No silks or tapestry, no fiddly antiques or thumbscrews or heavy drapes.

'You can move here,' Zoe said, and then she realised what she'd done: she'd seen something and automatically called for Nick to share it with her, trusting him to feel as she did.

'I'll get the groceries from the car,' she said, shrugging the feeling away.

'I'll get them.' Nick left, and she was in the house alone.

Except she wasn't alone. This house had Xenia in it: a Xenia whom Zoe had never seen, but whom, she realised, she had always known.

A staircase was set into one of the walls. Zoe climbed it up to a long hallway that was as strange and familiar to her as the rest of the house. The walls were painted green and they were lined with doors and framed photographs of trees and coastlines. Some of them were old sepia-toned pictures of the house years ago, probably when it had first been built, with people Zoe didn't know in long white dresses, formal suits, big hats.

She walked through the second door she came to and looked at the bedroom: a wooden double bed, a candlewick bedspread, an armchair, a roomy chest of drawers. *Nick and I could sleep here,* she thought, and had an instant picture of the two of them waking up together, the window open to let in the pine-scented morning sunlight. Every day waking up to his kind, sexy smile.

'Zoe?' The real Nick's voice cut through her tempting, dangerous daydream. She shut the door after her before going back down the stairs. Nick had brought both of their bags inside along with the groceries and the pigeon. Knowing him, he was feeling very pleased with himself for being the chivalrous gentleman carrying the big heavy luggage.

Then again, probably not. She'd learned he did these things without thinking, without calculating what he could get back or gain. And possibly, without even making any assumptions about her weakness or feminine unwillingness to carry heavy objects.

He was putting away the groceries in the kitchen, which was tucked into a corner of the open-plan room. 'Wow,' he said, his head in the refrigerator.

'What?'

'There's food in this fridge. Butter, ketchup, some eggs and cheese. And meat and vegetables in the freezer,' he added, checking it. He held up a package. 'Hot dogs. I thought you said Xenia didn't eat anything bigger than an oyster with her hands.'

'She was different up here,' Zoe said. 'Maybe she was here pretty recently and was planning to come back.'

'That would make sense. My father could have given her the letter to me while she was up here and she mailed it as soon as she got back to New York. I wonder why.'

'Maybe he didn't want you to know the postmark.'

'Could be, though that's strange if he was planning to come visit me soon anyway.'

'Maybe he wasn't planning it. He could have just decided yesterday.'

Nick closed the freezer with a snap. 'I shouldn't even bother trying to figure him out. Come on, didn't you want to go for a run?'

She considered Nick. Even the thought of his father got him agitated, now that he was so close to finding him. He'd been strung as tight as a wire since they'd got to the island, and, to tell the truth, she wasn't doing too great, either, if she was thinking about a life here with Nick that she would never have.

If his father came back tomorrow, all she was going to have with Nick was another night, and if she had anything to do with it, that night was going to be full of laughter and great sex. Because she wasn't going to find anyplace or anybody like this for a long time, if ever, and she wanted a memory or two.

'Yeah,' she said. 'Let's go and get it out of our system.'

Nick watched with amusement as Zoe poured the last bit of wine into his glass, remembering a time not so long ago when she would have taken it for herself.

'Thanks,' he said, chimed his glass with hers, and drank. The wine was excellent; probably too excellent to go with hot dogs and potato salad, but he was beginning to understand Zoe's natural mixture of unpretentiousness and true class.

He breathed in deep in contentment. The warm evening had mellowed gradually into cool night, but it was comfortable enough to sit here at the picnic table outside. Of course, being near Zoe brought heat of its own. Even something so simple as sitting together, eating a meal they'd prepared, turned him on, made him feel warm inside, as if he'd cupped his hands around one of the candles they'd taken from the house and drawn its heat deep into his bones.

'Thought you could do with an extra glass of wine after that workout,' Zoe said, her generous mouth in an impish smile.

'Are you implying I had trouble keeping up with you?' He hadn't, but she'd pushed him hard; pushed both of them hard, keeping a quick pace up some pretty steep climbs. Their bodies had worked together, as smoothly as when they made love. And then, when they were finished—

'Do you mean on the roads, or in the shower?'

'Both.' She raised an eyebrow at him, and he relived their post-exercise workout in the shower, both of them slick with sweat and soap and overcome with desire for each other. He'd remembered to bring a condom this time and they'd had sex, as hard and fast as their run, up against the tiled wall of the shower. Her cries had been sweeter than the sound of falling water.

He got up and moved around the table to sit on the other side, straddling the bench she sat on. 'We were together all the way.'

He pulled her towards him so that she leaned back against him, and began to rub the muscles of her neck and shoulders. Zoe made a low sound of contentment and relaxed under his hands.

Beyond the golden candlelight halo around the table, the night was velvet black and silver. They were far enough from the road not to hear any cars. In the silence as Nick massaged Zoe's back he heard a soft hooting from the forest surrounding them.

He didn't stop, but he pricked his ears. 'Hear that?'

'I hear nothing. After the Bronx, it's almost unnatural.'

'Listen.' It came again, a staccato tenor flute.

'I feel like I'm in a wildlife documentary. What is it, an owl?'

'A great horned owl.'

Another hoot, and Zoe said, 'It sounds eerie.'

'One of the most terrifying things I ever did involved hooting owls.'

'What happened? Did one of them mug you?'

He moved his hands down the column of her spine, kneading the muscles gently. She 'mmm'ed with pleasure.

'It wasn't far off from a mugging, actually. Owls are very territorial and I was doing a project mapping their territories in a certain area. It involved going out into the woods at night, with a map, a tape recorder, and a crash helmet.'

'And you say New Yorkers are weird.'

'I would walk around the area playing a recording of an owl hooting. Usually the owls hooted back. Then you'd mark it on the map. Unless you were near a nesting female. Then they'd hurtle down towards you and try to rip your head off with their talons.'

Zoe burst into laughter. 'You're kidding me, Boy Scout.'

'I'm serious. It was an amazing adrenaline rush: walking around a silent forest, looking up into the darkness in anticipation of a bird with a five-foot wingspan, huge talons and a curved beak swooping down out of nowhere.'

'You did this for fun?'

'I did it for conservation. But it was fun, too.' He reached her waist, and paused. 'Testing the boundaries to see at what point they'll be defended. It's not all that different from hanging out with you.'

Zoe laughed again, but this time it was less wholehearted. 'Yeah, I'm finding out all kinds of affinities with birds since meeting you.'

He kissed the warm side of her neck. 'You're different today, though.'

'Sometimes it gets tiring fighting.' She sighed, and he could feel the small tensing and relaxing of her body.

'I like the strong Zoe. And I like the defences-down Zoe, too.'

They both listened for the bird again, but it was quiet.

'I think I know what I'm going to do with Xenia's money,' Zoe said.

'What's that?'

'I don't need it. I like working. I think I might keep a little bit of it so that I can give up driving the cab and maybe set up my own exercise studio somewhere. The rest of it, I'm going to give away.'

'To who?'

She shrugged. 'It's not difficult to find people who need money. I'll give some of it to sports charities for inner-city kids, because I see a lot of those whose lives could really be turned around. Maybe I'll make you happy and give a bunch of it to wildlife conservation. I'm not sure yet, exactly. The one thing I do know is that I'm going to sell Xenia's houses and give the money to organisations for homeless runaways in New York.'

He smiled and kissed her on the neck to show his approval. But Zoe's reaction to Xenia's house here hadn't escaped Nick. 'You're going to sell all of the houses?'

She hesitated for the barest of split seconds. 'Yes.'

Nick used his hands on Zoe's waist to gently turn her around on the bench so that she faced him. It was going to ruin the tranquil mood between them, but he needed to ask this question. It seemed like a question he'd been asking more or less for most of his life.

'Zoe, why are you leaving?' he asked.

This time, she definitely stiffened under his loose grasp. Her blue eyes, so lively and expressive, turned from his.

'Like I said. I need to sort out all this money stuff. Fifty million dollars doesn't give itself away, you know.'

'You don't need to be in New York to write cheques. Or are you looking forward to seeing the gratitude of the people you give it to firsthand?'

At that, she did meet his gaze head-on. 'Don't be silly, I'm not giving it away for the gratitude. I don't want the money, and lots of other people could use it. Xenia gave it to me so that I could do what I liked. I'll give it away in her name.'

'So you don't need to be in New York to do that.'

She took a gulp of wine. 'Nick, I'm a New Yorker. The city made me what I am. I can't just pick up sticks and leave it.'

'You picked up sticks and went there in the first place. And your apartment in the Bronx didn't exactly look like you were putting down roots.'

Zoe snorted. 'Just because I'm no interior decorator you think that's a reason for me abandoning my whole life and coming up here to the middle of nowhere?'

'You can't fool me. You like Maine.'

'I like Dairy Queens, too, but I wouldn't go and live in one. What would I do up here?'

'Open an exercise studio, like you said. People in Maine exercise, too. You could link it in with some of the local sports—cross-country skiing, kayaking, rock-climbing.' He heard the owl again, and he gave her half a smile. 'Owl dodging.'

She didn't return his smile; instead she had the firm-chinned look he knew came with her defending her territory.

'Nick, five minutes ago you were all about my reconciling with my family. Now you're trying to convince me to drop everything and stay up here in the woods. Why are you trying to get me to stay?'

He'd had more arguments lined up, but that brought him up short, because he hadn't thought about any reasons. He just wanted her to. Badly.

'You'd be happy here, I think. You have that way of getting along with people but respecting their space that's valued in New England. And you seem more relaxed here, Zoe. More yourself. And I know I've only known you a little while,' he added quickly, because she looked as if she was going to interrupt him, 'but it's obvious. You're happier.'

'Yes, well, I'm also having great sex on a regular basis, which tends to relax a person, too. It's not like there's magic in the Maine air.'

'And there's another reason.' He took her hand in his and raised it to his mouth. He kissed each of her knuckles, then the sensitive inside of her wrist, and he heard her breath catch. 'Do you really want to walk away from this, Zoe?'

'Tonight? No.' She touched his hair with her other hand, a light butterfly stroke to push it back from his forehead. 'You're the sexiest thing I've ever seen by candlelight; I'd have to be insane.'

'So what makes you so sure you're going to want to walk away tomorrow?'

She shook her head. 'Oh, come on, you always knew I was leaving; this has been temporary from the start. This kind of—' she searched for the word, waving her hand in the air '—lust doesn't last for ever. It's great now, but it'll burn out and then here I am, up in the middle of nowhere while you're out climbing trees or whatever.'

'You don't know it'll burn out.'

'Nick, sex between us is like this wild, uncontrollable force. That can't last and I'm not going to throw away my life in New York and shack up with you because of it. I'd have thought you'd have figured that out by now. I don't change my life for anybody.'

'You wouldn't need to change anything, Zoe.'

She shook her head again, this time so vigorously her hair feathered around her face. 'Oh, yes, I would.'

'How?'

Zoe drank down the rest of her wine and stood up. 'If I have to explain it to you, there's no point.' She began stacking the plates they'd used for their dinner.

Nick watched her. He had no idea what to say. He'd never had to convince someone not to leave him before. Maybe he'd even chosen the girlfriends he had chosen, fragile and in need of protection, because he'd known they would never leave him.

And of course, with his father, he'd never had a chance to convince him not to leave.

Nick reached out and circled his hand around Zoe's wrist. 'Stop,' he said. 'Come here.'

For a split second it seemed as if she'd resist him, but then she relented. She stepped nearer to him, and he stood.

'Let me show you why you need to stay,' he said. He leaned

over and blew out the candles, and then he swept her into his arms and carried her into the darkness.

The difference, without the candlelight, wasn't that great and his eyes quickly adjusted to the starlight. He walked, sure-footed, towards the graceful ragged black shapes of the trees.

He liked carrying her. She didn't go limp or clingy; she relaxed into his arms and held on lightly, almost casually, as if she trusted him not to drop her. The side of her breast pressed against his chest and her hip bumped against his stomach not far above his crotch.

'Where are we going?' she asked.

'Just here, near the woods.' He knelt and set her down on the soft, even grass not far from where the trees started. He could smell her fresh scent mixed with the earthy pine.

'Why?'

'Because I want to make love to you, slowly, outdoors.'

'I won't argue with that.' She reached up and began to pull him down to her.

He stopped her with his hands on her arms. 'Not so fast. I said I wanted to make love to you. And I said I wanted to do it slowly.'

He lay down on his side next to her; in the shadowy light he could see her face as a silver and white glow. He took her chin between his fingers and thumb and stroked it, then savoured the softness of her cheek.

'You said that our sex was wild and out of control. And it has been, and that's been amazing. But I want to show you it doesn't always have to be that way. It can be slow and easy and gentle if we want it to be. It can be me giving pleasure to you instead of us both taking it. It can be—' he leaned forward and kissed her, lightly on the cheek where he'd just touched her, and then in the soft hollow underneath her ear '—whatever we want it to be.'

'Nick—'

He silenced her with a soft kiss on her mouth, and another. She tasted of wine and sweetness and with a small sigh she opened her lips to him.

Nick absolutely loved kissing this woman. Her mouth, so full of smart remarks and teasing smiles, melted under his. Her teeth were smooth and her tongue was a delicious flirt. The warm wetness of her mouth made him think of the warm wetness inside her, and need flared in him.

He ignored it, and concentrated on the textures of her mouth and the variations of her kiss, the way her breath feathered against his face and the way her body moved restlessly beside his. Although she was following his lead and kissing him unhurriedly, he could feel a tenseness in her body, maybe caused by desire, maybe by something else.

Maybe the something else that was going to lead her away from him.

'Relax, Zoe,' he whispered against her lips. He smoothed his hand down the length of her torso, from her graceful bare neck, between her breasts, to rest on her flat stomach. Through the material of her shirt he could feel her heart beating fast, and he could feel that her muscles were tight. He slipped his hand underneath her shirt and ran his fingertips in soothing circles around her navel. Her skin was incredibly smooth and amazingly precious and Nick knew what he had to do.

He wanted to love her with every part of his body, with every breath he took and every word he said. He wanted them to be together, truly together, here outside in the best place he could imagine. It was something he'd always wanted, even before he'd met her, because he loved being alone, but being together was something even better.

He wanted to make this time with her so perfect she wouldn't be able to bear to leave. And that meant getting her to open up to him.

He dropped another kiss on her lips, and then another, and then he said, 'Trust me, Zoe. I want you to put yourself in my hands. I want to take care of you and give you pleasure.' She began to say something and he kissed her again before she could, because he had one more word to say.

'Please.'

He held his breath and waited.

* * *

Nick Giroux and his husky sincerity. It got to her every time.

Zoe looked up into his face, blue and silver shadow. She could feel his warm breath on her face and his big body close. She couldn't quite see his eyes, but she remembered how he had looked the first time he had said 'please' to her, outside her great-aunt's apartment when he had been so sure that his father was inside that she had started to believe it, too.

She hadn't been able to resist him.

This time, he wasn't just asking her to give him what he wanted; he was asking her to give him what she wanted, more than anything in the world.

To be soft and trusting with Nick. To put herself in his hands and relax into the thrilling safety of his embrace. To abandon herself to the pleasure he gave her and feel it even more keenly because it was born out of emotion.

She'd been full of excuses earlier. Her desire for him wasn't ever going to burn out. Saying it would, though, was easier than admitting she was afraid that he'd get tired of her some day.

But tonight she could at least pretend that it was permanent.

His eyes were darker than the night around them. His hand on her belly was arousing and gentle. He smelled of the outdoors and of the wine they'd shared.

She took a deep breath, as full of him as she was. She let it out, letting her body relax.

'Okay,' she said.

She felt his smile even more than she could see it. Nick kissed her again with tenderness and passion and then, slowly, he began kissing a trail down her face and neck. His soft hair brushed against her skin. Zoe sighed and closed her eyes as she felt him parting her sweatshirt and kissing down over her chest, through her T-shirt. His mouth was warm even through the fabric, and she felt her breasts aching and nipples beading for his touch, but he avoided them, kissing between her breasts and over her ribs. When his lips touched the bare skin of her belly she nearly gasped.

She felt Nick raise his head and she opened her eyes to see him looking at her. 'The first time I touched you I was amazed at how soft your skin is,' he said. 'You're such a strong woman, and then you have skin like a new leaf.' He kissed her again on her stomach, and the heat of his tongue stroked into her belly button.

'You're very poetic,' she said, though it was more of a gasp because she was finding it difficult to breathe. The two of them had had sex again and again, in different positions and different ways, and his mouth tenderly touching her belly was one of the most erotic experiences she had ever had.

'Not usually.' He pushed her sweatshirt off her shoulders and slipped her T-shirt upwards. She helped him pull it over her head. She hadn't bothered with a bra after their shower and the night air on her bare breasts was both cold and delicious. When she lay back her skin was so sensitised by Nick's touch that she swore she could feel every strand of grass.

But for a minute he didn't touch her. He lay beside her, his body propped up on one arm, and she saw him looking at her. As if her body, laid half-naked here outdoors on the grass beneath the fragrant trees, was an offering to him.

As, God help her, it was.

'You're beautiful, Zoe,' he said to her, and she was never going to get sick of hearing that. 'Out here by starlight.'

'What's next, Boy Scout? You going to earn your romance badge by writing me a sonnet?'

His hand traced a slow line over her collar-bone; even in the silvery light she could see how much darker his skin was than hers. 'Why so resistant to compliments, Zoe? You must know I'm telling you the truth.'

She swallowed, because his words and his caress were too much. Nick stopped. He looked hard at her. 'Wait a minute. Don't you know?'

She tried to shrug, but couldn't quite manage it. 'I know you want me, and your poetry's very pretty, so—'

'No, Zoe, that's not what I'm talking about. I'm talking about how beautiful you are. Can't you see it for yourself? Hasn't anybody told you?'

Sexy, from her lovers and from drunks in the back of her cab.

Hot mama from her driving colleagues when she wore tight jeans and T-shirt. *Buff* from the guys in the gym. Once or twice, from her father, when she'd been dressed for parties in one of her sister's dresses: *pretty*. She'd cherished the word at the same time she'd disbelieved it.

And until now she would die rather than admit that it mattered to her.

'I haven't met many people who are as deluded as you.'

'Zoe.' Nick's voice held a warning, a reminder she'd agreed to be open.

'No,' she said quietly. 'Nobody has ever told me I was beautiful. I have beautiful sisters, I have a beautiful mother, and a beautiful great-aunt. I'm not. The only time I've ever felt beautiful—'

She paused, and then went on and said it, because, to tell the truth, she had hardly anything left to lose.

'The only time I've ever felt beautiful is when you look at me like you are right now.'

He let out a low laugh. 'Woman, you are the most gorgeous creature I've ever seen.' His tone was matter-of-fact, and more convincing than any poetic phrases. 'Let me show you.'

Nick bent his head to her and kissed her collar-bone, where he'd been touching her. His lips were as soft as the touch of the starlight on her skin. As if she were precious, as if he were reverent. His hair was just long enough to brush her chest, and it was another caress. He moved across, dipped his tongue into the hollow of her throat, and downward towards the swell of her breast. His hand, broad and warm, rested on her belly, lightly, but firmly enough to let her know that he was in control.

And she couldn't have done anything anyway. She was pinned by pleasure. Every kiss was a separate exquisiteness and she held her breath as he caressed and tasted the skin of her aching breast. Zoe threaded her fingers through his hair, not guiding him, just feeling him. When his tongue touched her nipple she jerked in a breath at the sensation.

She felt him smile. And then gently, so gently she couldn't tell his individual movements, just a slow circling of tongue and lips, he teased her nipple. The pleasure spread through her body, not only centred on her breast but all across her skin, between her legs, down to her toes.

Zoe tightened her fingers in his hair. He didn't vary his unhurried movement, but he stroked a thumb across her belly, and the small caress was so wonderful she shuddered.

With a final small kiss he lifted his head from her breast. 'You're beautiful, Zoe,' he whispered, and she felt his breath warm against her wet, sensitive skin before she felt the cool evening air. Her nipple hardened still more, and it would have been painful if it hadn't felt so good.

Then he put his mouth on her other breast and it got even better.

Those hands, his hands that healed and comforted and saved, held her more carefully than she'd ever been touched before. She lost track of time. Somewhere above the stars were wheeling around the earth; somewhere below the world was turning towards tomorrow.

And tomorrow, she would leave.

But right now she thought she could feel for ever.

Nick raised his head again and although she'd been looking at the stars she met his eyes. 'Do you believe me yet?' he asked.

Nick, I think I would even believe you if you said you loved me.

The thought was so strong she didn't dare to open her mouth in case she said it.

'I'm going to have to try harder,' Nick said.

CHAPTER FOURTEEN

ZOE WATCHED NICK kneel beside her and draw her sweatpants down her legs and off. In the darkness he was a familiar and perfect outline, though her eyes had adjusted to the starlight enough so that she could make out his features.

She hadn't bothered putting on underwear, either. She lay totally naked on the grass underneath the open sky and again Nick looked at her for a long moment before he said or did anything.

The first sound he made surprised her. He sighed.

'Nick?'

He laid a gentle hand on her hip, as if he knew she'd meant to sit up. 'I was just thinking how strange it is that I've spent so much of my life outdoors and I've never made love outside like this.'

'Never?'

She could see him shake his head. 'Weird, isn't it? I just never found a woman I wanted to share this with.' He paused, and although she couldn't see exactly where he was looking, Zoe could feel his gaze on her body. 'I love seeing you like this, naked in the open air.'

'You could get naked, too. We could do an Adam and Eve.'

'Not yet.' He ran one hand down the length of her leg and again Zoe shivered. 'But it is like that. Like it's just you and me, and all the trees and animals, and nobody else.' His hand stroked back up her leg. 'Nobody else at all.'

He bent and kissed her thigh. After minutes without his mouth on her, it was almost shockingly warm. Without consciously planning to, Zoe opened her legs and Nick shifted himself so that he was kneeling between them.

His hands and mouth explored her legs, from hip to toe, every touch soft and caring, and Zoe heard Nick and felt Nick and touched Nick and she heard and felt and touched the outdoors, too. The sky, the breeze, the owl in the distance and the other sounds of animals. In Nick's world, she was beautiful and cherished and even the ground was a welcoming bed.

He kissed her inner thigh and, though she'd been relaxed and patient, she couldn't help lifting her hips. 'Touch me, please, Nick.'

She heard him make a deep sound of amusement and satisfaction. His breath feathered against the yearning flesh between her legs, and that wasn't enough, either.

But he held her still with hands on her hips and made his own slow way. A kiss in the crease of her thigh where her leg met her body. Another, lower down. And then the liquid heat of his tongue, parting her and tasting her, and Zoe closed her eyes in ecstasy and whispered 'Nick' to the night air.

The man was patient, and he was in no hurry. It would have been maddening if it weren't so damn good. He swirled his tongue around her clitoris with the most delicate of touches and Zoe felt as if she were melting. His breath was almost as much of a caress as his tongue and lips.

'Nick,' she said again, louder this time, and she felt, as well as heard his sound of satisfaction. It was a male sound, a sound of conquest, and she didn't mind because his voice vibrated against her crotch and over her nerve endings through her entire body.

And besides, she was his.

She clutched his hair with one hand and dug the fingers of the other into the grass beside her. In the haziness of her passion it felt as if Nick were everywhere. He stroked her with his mouth, and the cool breeze on her over-sensitised breasts and skin was him, too. Slowly, slowly, he traced his finger around her and then slid it inside her, a fraction of an inch at a time.

That was it. Her muscles clenched around him and though his

touches had been gentle her orgasm was violent, pounding and overwhelming. The stars blurred and the world stopped and Zoe arched her back, hit the ground with her fist, and heard herself gasping Nick's name over and over.

He gave her a last, lingering lick, wringing another round of pleasure from her, and then he slid up her body so his face was even with hers.

'I love it when you do that,' he said.

'I'm partial to it myself,' she answered, dizzy and breathless.

He kissed her and she could taste herself on him, which was somehow doubly erotic. Then he sat up beside her and began removing his clothes.

Zoe watched him. Her limbs were languid and heavy, still tingling with her orgasm.

His chest in the starlight was a plane of rippled shadow, and his legs were long and perfect. When he moved to reach in the pocket of his jeans she could see the silhouette of his erection.

She didn't move—she couldn't—but desire stirred inside. No matter how many climaxes she had, no matter how satisfied she was, she always wanted more of Nick.

She heard the crinkling of a packet and knew he had found a condom and was putting it on. Her hands remembered how it felt to smooth latex over his rigid length; her body remembered how it felt to have Nick inside her. She would never get enough of him, even if she had the chance to. She bit her lip with longing.

'You're prepared,' she murmured.

'More than,' he said, and leaned forward and gathered her into his arms. She let him position her in his lap, so they were sitting facing each other with her legs around his hips. His legs were firm underneath hers and her breasts pressed against his chest. Between her legs, she could feel the hot weight of his penis.

He kissed her again. She looped her arms around his neck, using his broad shoulders and his strength to steady herself. Nick took hold of her hips in his big hands and guided her carefully over him and downwards. His penis slid into her, inch by tantalising inch, while Zoe looked into his dark eyes.

When she had taken all of him in he stopped and held her still in his arms. Zoe could feel him wonderfully embedded in her, pulsing and alive, his heartbeat fast against hers. For all his calm steadiness he seemed to be having as much trouble breathing as she was.

She tensed her thighs, wanting to move on him, to feel the friction of him thrusting in and out of her, but he tightened his grip on her so that she couldn't budge.

'Look at the sky,' he whispered to her, and that was his final step towards owning all of her world. Her body was surrounded by him and penetrated by him, her breath full of him, his taste on her lips and his voice in her ears. For a second all she could do was stare back into his eyes.

'At the sky,' he said again, and she tore her gaze away to look upwards. Millions and billions of stars, every one of them a tiny world. They formed constellations she didn't know.

Her breath caught in her throat.

It was beautiful. And she was never going to see them again. Because Nick was her world now, but after tomorrow she would be gone. And they didn't have stars like this in New York.

Then Nick moved. And the loss that had flooded her didn't go away, but retreated back into her mind and her heart and burned there, while Zoe's body revelled in the incredible pleasure Nick was giving her. He moved subtly, steadily, slow strokes that ignited every nerve inside her. The base of his penis rubbed against her clitoris and built up the same ecstasy he'd already given her with his mouth. And her nipples brushed the hard wall of his chest, and her thighs clenched and trembled around his waist, and her mouth kissed him and kissed him while she completely lost her mind.

She didn't feel her orgasm coming; it just happened, as if it had never stopped. As she shuddered around him Nick held her still tighter, his movements barely quickening, until he suddenly raised her nearly off him and then brought her down fast, filling her so hard and completely that she gasped and cried out at the same time he pulsed his release.

'Zoe,' he murmured, pushed her hair back from her face, and tucked her head underneath his chin as they breathed together, sweat cooling on their bodies.

She had never felt so precious.

Here, held by him with their hearts beating in time, she had one thought. *I love you.*

It almost seemed safe enough to say it. And she would never get another chance.

Zoe opened her mouth. The words were so momentous and strange. She practised one, moving her lips and tongue without giving it voice.

Love.

A sharp pin pricked her thigh. 'Ouch,' she said, and slapped at her leg.

Nick chuckled and she felt it through her whole body. 'Think you got bitten by an early black fly.' He touched her leg where she'd swatted, identifying the small already-swollen bump. 'It's not quite the season yet, or we wouldn't be able to be out here.'

She could still say it, but the moment of safety had passed. 'Insects,' she said instead. 'I knew there was a downside to the boondocks.'

'Black flies are the unofficial Maine state bird,' Nick said. He shifted her weight off him, slipping out of her. She felt the loss of the bond as if it were more than just flesh.

He helped her stand up; her legs were stiff. Nick kissed her and picked her up again easily. 'Let's go inside,' he said, striding towards the house. 'There are screens to keep out the bugs.'

Even without being joined, there was a comfortable intimacy between them. She laughed when Nick kicked the door open with his foot in imitation of some passionate romance-novel hero and it swung back and hit him in the butt when they were halfway through it. He climbed the stairs without any strain at all and without looking around went straight into one of the bedrooms.

They were halfway to the bed before Zoe realised it was the bedroom she'd looked into earlier, where she'd had visions of them sleeping together, limbs entwined. He'd chosen the same room she had for the two of them.

'This is——' she started to say, then stopped.

'What is it?' Nick asked, setting her carefully on the bed.

A coincidence. 'A nice room,' she said, and pulled him down to lie beside her.

Still, as they snuggled underneath the quilt and into each other, it felt like more than a coincidence. It felt like some kind of sign, as if the future she'd thought about with Nick could maybe be more than an impossible dream.

It was darker in the house than it had been outside. Zoe hooked one leg around Nick's thigh, nestling closer to him. She ran her hand through his hair and over his features. The textures of silky hair, sandpapery chin, hard jaw, the tender skin around his eyes. When her fingers passed over his lips he kissed them.

Imagine doing this every single night. Right here in this bed, which yielded to their bodies as if they had slept in it for years.

There was a distant rustle and then a crash from outside the window. Zoe stopped moving. 'What's that?'

'Raccoons,' Nick answered, still completely relaxed and holding her. 'They're after what's left of our dinner now we're inside.' He let out a long, contented breath. 'I don't care. I could lie like this with you for ever.'

It was so much like what she'd been thinking—not the raccoons, but the part about being together for ever. The risk she'd avoided ten minutes ago, the momentous words, came back to her.

She could stay here with him. She could tell him she loved him.

Lying with him here, like this, she could almost believe he loved her, too.

'So, Boy Scout,' she said lightly, letting her fingers walk over his chest, 'tell me something. You ever been in love?'

He didn't answer for a moment. Outside, there was another rustle and a crunching sound. Zoe ignored it and waited.

'I don't think so,' he said, slowly. 'I've been involved with women, and I think I've believed I was in love once or twice. But I wasn't.'

Her heart was gripped in a fist and squeezed, hard.

No. He wasn't in love with her. He was a good man, a kind man, a passionate man. And what was between them was goodness and kindness and passion.

Problem was, that wasn't enough for her, not from Nick. Not enough to make her stay.

'I—' He hesitated again, and then let out a breath and continued. 'I wondered if I was too much like my father.'

Her heart throbbed again. Nick's voice held pain and doubt.

Zoe forgot about the rest of her life. She could deal with that tomorrow. Tonight, Nick needed goodness and kindness back.

'You're not like your father,' she said.

'I am, in some ways. In maybe a lot of ways. I'm committed to my job, and I think I could be committed to a woman and a family. But maybe I'm wrong. I've never tried it. Maybe if I were in the same situation as my dad, I would walk out, too.'

'How do you feel about seeing him tomorrow?' she asked quietly.

'Honestly? I'm scared, Zoe.' He tightened his grip on her. 'God, I'm only saying this because it's dark and I'm with you. But my sister said he was all right when she met him. I keep on thinking that maybe if he's not such a bad guy, maybe it was me. Maybe I deserved to be left.'

The words nearly made her gasp. They were like a jackknife to her belly.

Because tomorrow, she planned to leave, just like that. She'd been thinking about how much it would hurt her.

For the first time, she saw that it would hurt Nick, too.

Not because he loved her. But because it was part of the pattern that had hurt him in the past. Because he'd asked her to stay, for whatever reason, and she wouldn't. As soon as he was reunited with his father, she was out of there.

She drew him closer to her, laying his head on her breast. She wrapped her body around him and she held him tight. Just for now.

'You don't deserve to be left,' she whispered.

* * *

Nick woke up alone.

He stretched his arm out to the side, where Zoe had lain last night, her body wrapped around his. There was an indentation on the pillow, but the sheets were cold.

He sat up. Light streamed through the window and an automatic calculation told him it was past ten in the morning. He felt refreshed; he remembered falling asleep with Zoe in his arms and he didn't think he'd ever slept so well. He also had a hard-on, which wasn't very surprising given that he'd dreamed about Zoe all night, too.

You don't deserve to be left. It was amazing how much those words meant to him. It was something, incredibly, that nobody had ever said to him before. Much like, he supposed, how nobody had ever told Zoe she was beautiful.

And if Zoe didn't think he deserved to be left, then she was going to stay.

Nick smiled, sat up, and stretched. Last night had been amazing. He'd shared something with Zoe that he'd never felt with another woman, but that he realised he'd been wanting all his life. And today, with her staying, was going to be even better.

The clothes he'd worn last night were neatly folded over the back of a chair. Zoe must have gone outside this morning and picked them up—some time ago, too, because when he got up and touched them they weren't damp or cold. He got dressed, noticing with a smile the grass stains on the knees of his jeans.

He hummed as he went downstairs. He could smell coffee and toast. His stomach grumbled. It was looking like a perfect morning: first he'd have some breakfast with Zoe, and then he'd see about doing something about reviving that hard-on he'd woken up with.

Zoe was sitting at the kitchen table, spinning something in her hand. She had a cup of coffee in front of her and her hair was bright in the morning sun. The pigeon in its cage was on the table beside her. She didn't look up when he came down the stairs, seemingly lost in her own thoughts.

'Morning, gorgeous,' he said. Zoe blinked and raised her

head. There was something in her eyes, probably surprise at being disturbed from her daydream. He crossed the room and kissed her on her cheek.

'Morning.' Her voice was cheerful, without a sign of whatever expression had been on her face. 'You're late. I thought you park ranger types had to be up with the sun.'

'I've never slept so well in my life.' He poured himself coffee from the pot and put a couple of slices of bread into the toaster. 'I thought you heiress types never did anything but lounge in bed eating bonbons.'

'I've been exploring. And cleaning up. Those raccoons really have a talent for demolition.'

'You should see what happens when the bears get involved.' He sat beside her and pushed a strand of hair back from her face. 'It's not a good idea to let them get used to eating human food. I should have gotten up and scared them away last night, but I preferred to stay in bed with you.'

Zoe shrugged. 'Well, it won't kill them for one night.'

Nick noticed that the object in her hand was a set of car keys. 'What are those?'

'Xenia has a four-by-four in her garage. She must have kept it for using up here. I found the keys hanging in a kitchen cupboard.'

'Well, that'll be handy for you. Unless you were planning to have a New York cab shipped up here to make you feel more at home.' The toast popped up and Nick got up. He slathered the toast with butter and had eaten a piece in four bites by the time he sat back down.

Zoe was still toying with the keys. 'I also found a path through the woods that leads to your father's trailer. He probably uses it to come to work.'

Nick had nearly polished off the other piece of toast. He put the last bite down. 'Is he back yet?'

'He wasn't when I checked, but that was about two hours ago.'

Funny how he'd been so happy about being with Zoe that he'd completely forgotten the main reason why he was here.

'I'll go over in a little while,' he said. 'Meanwhile, I was very disappointed when I woke up and you weren't still in bed, because I'd planned to begin this day by having sex with you. It's not too late to go start again, though.' He stood, smiling, and held out his hand to her.

She stood, too, but she didn't take his hand. 'You're disappointing me, Giroux. You're going to give up your obsession just like that, after driving all those miles in a circle? I thought you'd be down that path like a shot.'

She was right. He had to see his father; putting it off wouldn't change anything. He nodded. 'All right, let's go, and we can go back to bed later.'

She didn't return his smile, either. His melted away. 'Zoe? Something wrong?'

'It's just the tension. Waiting for your dream to come true. Come on, let's go find him and get this done.'

He followed her out of the house, banging the screen door behind them, and across the lawn. The path was broad enough for a four-wheeler or a snowmobile in the winter; Nick thought that his dad probably had one, or both, in his shed. It was certainly wide enough for him and Zoe to walk side by side, but she was striding ahead of him.

He quickened his steps to catch up with her. 'Zoe, what's wrong?'

'I told you, everything's fine.' In the shafts of full sunlight filtering through the pine trees he could see that her face was pale.

'Did you sleep?'

'Not so great.' She wasn't looking at him, either, just walking fast. 'It's a lot shorter to your dad's house by this path than by the road.'

'How long have you been up?'

'A while. I had a run. Hard to see the sunrise with all these trees so I went back towards town.'

Disquiet rolled inside Nick's stomach. 'There's something you're not telling me.'

Zoe stopped and held up her hand. 'Listen. I think that's your dad.'

He could hear the sound of a car ahead of them through the

trees. They'd gone far enough so he reckoned that the path ended in a hundred yards or so. He couldn't see the car, but it sounded as if it was pulling up in what would be his father's driveway.

He strode forward, the noise of the car louder than the noise of the leaves and twigs underfoot, and the noise of his breath and heartbeat louder than any of it. Within seconds he could see the car through the trees, a beat-up blue pick-up. It stopped and Nick, after a couple more steps, stopped, too, still on the path just inside the tree line, half behind a bush and far enough away that he wouldn't be immediately visible from the pick-up. He stood and watched.

The driver's side opened and a man stepped out. He was wearing jeans and a flannel shirt and he was Nick's dad.

Nick didn't have to think about it, or catalogue features to recognise him. It wasn't the instantaneous connection he'd wondered about, either. He just knew this man was his dad as he knew that a car was a car and the sun was the sun. His dad was tall and had brown hair with some grey in it, and he reached back into the truck and pulled out a plastic carrier bag.

'That's him,' Zoe said beside him. He hadn't heard her come up but he'd known she was there anyway, in the same way that he knew who this man was.

'Yeah.'

'Good. I'm glad you found him. That makes this easier.' Zoe kissed his cheek, and then stepped back. 'Good luck, Nick. It was nice knowing you.'

She turned and walked away.

CHAPTER FIFTEEN

IT MADE SO little sense that Nick stood there for a moment as his brain stuttered. Only the sight of Zoe walking quickly away from him brought him back to life.

From his father's driveway, he heard the truck door shut. He ran after Zoe and grabbed her shoulder, turning her around to face him.

'What?' he said.

'I said good luck and it was nice knowing you. Go talk to your father, Nick, it's what you want to do.'

'And what are you doing?'

'I'm going back to New York.'

He stared at her. Her jaw was set and her body was tense. Disbelief was making him numb, but already that numbness was fraying, giving way to something else.

'You're going back to New York and that's all you have to say to me? Good luck? It was nice to know me?'

She pressed her lips together. 'You're right. I should have also said goodbye, and if you're ever in New York again, give me a call.'

She tried to turn away from him again, but he didn't let her. 'Why?' he asked, his voice hoarse.

'I told you my reasons last night, remember? I've got a life in New York, and I like that life, and I'm going back to it.'

'Zoe, that's bull and you know it is.'

'Well, it's my bull.' She stuck her chin out still more.

Everything he had said to her last night, everything they had shared. It had made no difference. He had had the chance to stop her from going, and he'd failed.

He held on to her shoulders tight, as if that would make up for what he hadn't been able to do.

'And nothing we did together made any difference at all? Not even last night? That meant nothing to you?'

She jerked her shoulders under his hands. 'Nick, let me go.'

'Answer me, Zoe.'

'Nick, if you don't let me go, I can force you to do it, and that's not going to be fun for either of us.'

She had that 'don't-mess' edge in her voice. Nick took his hands off her.

'Thank you.' She turned around and started walking off again.

He most definitely wasn't numb now. Anger flared in him, and he ran past her and stood in front of her, his hands on his hips, his legs spread wide, blocking her way.

'You're lying,' he said.

'You can believe what you want, Nick, but I'm going home. Let me by.'

'I know what this is really about. It's you. You're doing the same thing you always do, pushing people away, pushing me away, because you're scared to trust anybody or open up.'

She shrugged. She was meeting his eyes now, but he couldn't see any emotion there. Her blankness made him even madder.

'You're running away,' he said fiercely. 'You said you wanted to make other people's lives better but you can't even take a risk for yourself. You think you're tough, Zoe, but you're not. Strong people don't run away. Only cowards.'

This time, there was some emotion. Her eyes narrowed and her face got harder.

'Congratulations, Nick,' she said. 'You finally got it. I'm a screw-up. Now goodbye.'

She stepped off the path, into the undergrowth, trying to walk around him.

'You don't care about anything except for your own safe life,'

Nick threw at her, beyond furious, not thinking about what he was saying. 'You don't care what your great-aunt wanted for you or how your parents feel about you or about taking any responsibility. You don't even care that I love you.'

Zoe stopped dead still and Nick realised what he had said at the same time he saw all the blood drain from her face.

He put his hand to his forehead and felt how his own skin was hot.

He loved her. He'd meant it.

'No,' she said, and her lips were nearly as white as her cheeks. 'You're right. I don't care.'

He couldn't say anything else. Her words were a sucker punch in the gut. He stared at her and she looked back at him with that maddening, impenetrable defiance.

Faintly, from the end of the path, he heard a car door slam and the sound of his father's truck starting up again.

'Go see your father,' Zoe said. 'He's the person you're really looking for.'

She kicked through a wad of leaves that stood in her way and walked past him and away. Again.

Finally and for ever.

Nick turned and ran back towards the noise of the truck. His blood pounded in his head. His father, he could get through to. His father had abandoned his family. His father was wrong and his father, unlike Zoe, owed him love because his father had created him.

Zoe had only changed him.

He burst into the clearing and ran towards the truck, words warring in his head, the words he'd thought about saying to his father for years.

A real man doesn't walk out on his family. A real man wouldn't let his wife and children scrape for money and live on their own. A real man takes care of the people he's committed to. He loves them and protects them no matter what.

I called her a coward.

Nick stopped running, because all of his energy seemed to have suddenly drained away. He stood on the driveway, pulled forward, pulled back, as unable to move by himself as a rooted oak.

The truck had been backing up but it braked. Nick heard the ignition switch off. The door opened and his father stepped down from the cab.

'Hi, Nicky,' said Eric Giroux.

Nick hadn't heard the pet name since he'd been a boy. He watched his father walking towards him and saw a faint limp, a weather-beaten face, more signs of time.

None of his rehearsed words came to him. His anger seemed to be lying in pieces at his feet, leaving him hollow.

'Nick,' he said finally. 'I'm called Nick now, Dad.'

'Oh. Yeah.' Eric stopped in front of Nick. He started to put out his hand, and then seemingly thought better of it and dropped it. Nick didn't make a move to touch him. A hug was too intimate, a handshake too distant for this man who had held him as a baby and taught him to fish and disappeared.

Eric was a little shorter than Nick and more wiry. He nodded quickly once, his eyes casting around, and Nick could see how awkward he felt.

'I stopped at your house,' Eric said. 'Your sister says you were out looking for me.'

'I went to New York,' Nick said, and the pain that shot through him was almost unbelievable because he'd found Zoe in New York. He closed his eyes and said the first thing to distract him from the hurt. 'Why'd you write to me, Dad?'

'Well, I got talking to the lady I work for yonder,' Eric began, and Nick opened his eyes.

'Xenia Drake?'

'Ayuh. I been working for her for years, and we got talking. She asked me if I had kids and she has a way, you know, of drawing you out. I told her about you and Kitty and she said she had this niece who was special, and she got to talking about her will and it made me think, you know.' He stuffed his hands in the pockets of his jeans, an action that made him seem smaller. 'I never saw you for so many years but I heard about what you been doing, a ranger here on the island, and I'm real proud. Real proud.'

For a second he met Nick's eyes, and then he shifted his gaze back to the trees behind him. Nick felt as if he'd been given a gift he hadn't expected and didn't know what to do with.

'So I wrote a letter and asked Miss Drake to mail it for me somewhere. I didn't want to mail it from Southwest Harbour, because I didn't want you to feel you had to, you know, come visit if you didn't want to.'

'Xenia told you about Zoe and that made you decide to write to me,' Nick said, and Eric nodded.

Zoe and his father, each leading him towards the other without even knowing it. And now Zoe was driving away. Down Seal Cove Road, back onto Route 3, onto the mainland and towards the south.

And now he had his father. Except this man wasn't the man he'd wanted all these years. He was a familiar stranger, someone Nick couldn't even be angry with.

Zoe was everything he wanted even though he'd never known it, and the last words he'd said to her had been in anger. He'd even told her he loved her in anger.

He remembered the darkness of the bedroom last night, how she'd asked him if he'd ever been in love. At the time he'd taken it at face value, as a question about his past, not thinking about why she'd asked.

He hadn't known yet that she was the answer. He'd thought she was going to stay.

'Why'd you leave?' he burst out, and, though that was the question he'd been waiting so long to ask, he didn't want the answer from this man in front of him. But Eric Giroux was the only person he had to ask, any more.

Eric's work boots shuffled in the dirt. 'I don't know,' he said. 'I just left, I guess. It was easier alone. And then it was too late to go back.'

Nick looked at his father, really looked at him. Not to see how he'd changed from sixteen years ago, not to look for resemblances or memories. Just to see who he was: a middle-aged man, strong in body, uncomfortable with words, who had made a decision, maybe a mistake, half a lifetime ago and had been alone ever since.

Nick's feet and mind came unstuck and the hollowness inside him filled with urgency. She was going. She might be gone already.

'I'm in love with a woman,' Nick said, 'and I've got to go find her.'

He was starting to run for the path even before he registered Eric's, 'Oh, ayuh.'

But the voice stopped him. There was something defeated in his father, something, in all his thoughts about him, Nick had never imagined would be there.

Nick ran back to his father, and put his hand on his shoulder. The gesture of companionship, a man to another man.

'I'll be back,' Nick told him, and then he was sprinting.

She couldn't open the garage door.

It wasn't heavy. She'd opened it earlier this morning. But her arms wouldn't work and her breath wouldn't come and she could barely see anything because any minute now she was going to erupt into big girly tears.

Dear God, she thought. *He loves me.*

Even last night when she'd been caught up in her for ever fantasies, she hadn't thought that she'd be able to believe it. Not that he really could love her. But the way he'd said it, angrily as part of his accusations. Everything else had been the truth and so she knew that this was the truth, too.

He loved her and she loved him and she'd known it even while she'd walked away from him. Because she was too scared to stay.

And now she was too scared to leave.

'Damn,' she said, and dropped the keys to the four-by-four on the ground.

Her tears started to fall as soon as she was back on the path towards Eric Giroux's house. She ran ahead, letting them fall without wiping them from her eyes.

She recognised Nick running towards her from the way he

moved and from the way she felt. Zoe didn't pause in her running or her crying. She went straight into his arms and buried her face in his shirt and breathed him in deep, through sobs.

He held her tight. 'I thought you'd be gone,' he said into her hair.

'I couldn't,' she said, and then lifted her head so she could look him in the eyes. Her face was smeared with tears and her nose and eyes were probably red and swollen and she did not care.

'I love you,' she said. 'I couldn't go because I love you and I've loved you since the minute I first saw you.'

'Zoe.' He squeezed her so tight she could barely breathe, and kissed her hair, her forehead, in between words. 'I'm sorry I said those things to you. I didn't mean them. I was angry and hurt. You're not a coward. You're the strongest, most wonderful woman I know.'

'I am a coward.'

He stopped kissing her and looked her in the face. Her nose was running, but she didn't want to take her hands off him so she sniffed before she spoke.

'If I were strong, I would have gone. I'll lose myself if I stay with you, Nick. That's why I was leaving. I'll rely on you and I'll live in your world and I'll never be independent again. I've been fighting against it ever since I met you.'

She sniffed again. 'But I can't fight any more. It hurts too much.' She pressed her head back against his chest and listened to his heartbeat and the air pumping in and out of his lungs. His arms around her felt like something she'd been waiting her whole life for. They *were* something she'd been waiting her whole life for.

'Zoe,' he said again, and he raised her chin with one of his hands. 'This isn't my world. It's ours. Remember last night, you and me and the stars?'

'Don't forget the raccoons.'

'I was running back here to you and if you'd been gone, I was going to get in my truck and drive after you all the way to New York and set up my tent outside your door if I had to and wait for you to talk to me. I'll go to your world if you want, Zoe. It doesn't matter to me. You're the important thing.'

'But you hate New York.'

'And you love Maine. But I don't care, if you want to be stubborn I can be stubborn, too. I'll wait you out, Zoe Drake. Because I want to rely on you just as much as you want to rely on me, and if you can't see that you really are an idiot.'

He wiped the tears from her eyes with his gentle hand. It was a protective gesture, but it didn't make her feel weak. It made her feel loved. She remembered curling around him at night, stroking his hair.

'I'll even do step aerobics,' he said, and at that she couldn't help a smile.

'We are going to drive each other crazy,' she said.

'But making up is going to be great.'

He kissed her and she kissed him back and in the solid reality of his embrace she began to see how they could be equals in passion, equals in love, equals in everything. Together.

'I love you, Zoe,' he said when they parted.

'I love you, Nick.'

'Please stay.'

She nodded. 'I'll try it.'

They shared a smile and Zoe could not remember ever feeling so happy in her life.

'Let's live in Xenia's house,' she said.

His extra squeeze and kiss let her know that he liked the idea. 'My father will be our neighbour.'

She furrowed her brow. 'Oh, I'm sorry, Nick. I wanted to be there when you met him.'

'I wanted you to be there, too. But you will.'

'What's he like?'

'He's all right.' Nick threaded his fingers with hers. 'Come on. Let's go meet him.'

REQUEST YOUR FREE BOOKS!

HARLEQUIN *Presents* ®

PASSION GUARANTEED SEDUCTION

2 FREE NOVELS
PLUS 2
FREE GIFTS!

YES! Please send me 2 FREE Harlequin Presents® novels and my 2 FREE gifts (gifts are worth about $10). After receiving them, if I don't wish to receive any more books, I can return the shipping statement marked "cancel". If I don't cancel, I will receive 6 brand-new novels every month and be billed just $4.05 per book in the U.S. or $4.74 per book in Canada, plus 25¢ shipping and handling per book and applicable taxes, if any*. That's a savings of close to 15% off the cover price! I understand that accepting the 2 free books and gifts places me under no obligation to buy anything. I can always return a shipment and cancel at any time. Even if I never buy another book, the two free books and gifts are mine to keep forever.

106 HDN ERRW   306 HDN ERRL

Name	(PLEASE PRINT)	
Address		Apt. #
City	State/Prov.	Zip/Postal Code

Signature (if under 18, a parent or guardian must sign)

Mail to the Harlequin Reader Service:
IN U.S.A.: P.O. Box 1867, Buffalo, NY 14240-1867
IN CANADA: P.O. Box 609, Fort Erie, Ontario L2A 5X3

Not valid to current subscribers of Harlequin Presents books.

Want to try two free books from another line?
Call 1-800-873-8635 or visit www.morefreebooks.com.

* Terms and prices subject to change without notice. N.Y. residents add applicable sales tax. Canadian residents will be charged applicable provincial taxes and GST. This offer is limited to one order per household. All orders subject to approval. Credit or debit balances in a customer's account(s) may be offset by any other outstanding balance owed by or to the customer. Please allow 4 to 6 weeks for delivery. Offer available while quantities last.

Your Privacy: Harlequin Books is committed to protecting your privacy. Our Privacy Policy is available online at www.eHarlequin.com or upon request from the Reader Service. From time to time we make our lists of customers available to reputable third parties who may have a product or service of interest to you. If you would prefer we not share your name and address, please check here. ☐

HP08